ALSO BY GRAHAM SALISBURY

GRAHAM SALISBURY

NIGHT OF THE
HOWLING
DOGS

LAUREL-LEAF
BOOKS

Published by Laurel-Leaf
an imprint of Random House Children's Books
a division of Random House, Inc.
New York

Originally published in hardcover in the United States by Wendy Lamb Books,
New York, in 2007. This edition published by arrangement with Wendy Lamb Books.

Laurel-Leaf and colophon are registered trademarks of Random House, Inc.

Visit us on the Web! www.randomhouse.com/teens

Educators and librarians, for a variety of teaching tools, visit us at
www.randomhouse.com/teachers

The Library of Congress has cataloged the hardcover edition of this work as follows:
Salisbury, Graham.
Night of the howling dogs : a novel / Graham Salisbury
p. cm.
Summary: In 1975, eleven Boy Scouts, their leaders, and some new friends camping at Halape,
Hawaii, find their survival skills put to the test when a massive earthquake strikes, followed by
a tsunami.
ISBN: 978-0-385-73122-5 (trade)—ISBN: 978-0-385-90146-8 (glb)
[1. Earthquakes—Hawaii—Fiction. 2. Tsunamis—Fiction. 3. Survival—Fiction. 4. Boy Scouts
of America—Fiction. 5. Camping—Fiction. 6. Interpersonal relations—Fiction. 7. Hawaii—
History—20th Century—Fiction.] I. Title.
PZ7.S15225Nig 2007
[Fic]—dc22   2007007054

ISBN: 978-0-440-23839-3 (pbk.)

RL: 5.6
March 2009
Printed in the United States of America
10 9 8 7 6

First Laurel-Leaf Edition

FOR MY COUSIN, TIM TWIGG-SMITH,
AS SOLID AS THEY COME

FOR THE FAMILY OF FISHERMAN MICHAEL CRUZ,
THE FAMILY OF DR. JAMES A. MITCHEL,
AND BOY SCOUT TROOP 77,
HILO, HAWAII,
1975

FOR MY TWO EAGLE SCOUT SONS,
ALEX SALISBURY AND ZACH SALISBURY—
AND MY EAGLE SCOUT NEPHEW,
NICK COWAN—
YOU MAKE ME PROUD.

IT KEPT COMING AND COMING . . .

—"HAWAII REPORT,"
THE HONOLULU ADVERTISER,
DECEMBER 2, 1975

NIGHT OF THE
HOWLING
DOGS

1
HILO, HAWAII

At 3:20 in the morning I woke and rode my bike down the old coast road to Casey Bellows's house. I followed the broken white line in the middle of the road, ghostly gray under the stars. Every now and then somebody's yard light blinked from the jungle, but mostly it was black as tar. The only living thing I saw was a toad that sprang out and leaped across the road. Scared the spit out of me.

By 3:45 I stood with Casey by the old Ford van in his yard, our camping gear strewn around us in the yellow glow from the garage. We both wore T-shirts, shorts, and hiking boots strong enough to take a beating. My boots were new, and stiff. I hoped they wouldn't give me blisters.

I was wide awake now, and could feel the anticipation jumping inside me. This time tomorrow we'd be sleeping under a volcano in a place so remote even rats had no business going there.

I looked east, out toward the black ocean across the coast road. No hint of dawn. "Jeese," I said, wiping the back of my neck. "Already I'm sweating."

Casey grunted, securing his sleeping bag to his backpack. "Wait till you feel the heat where we're going . . . you'll wish you were dead."

"You always come up with just the right thing to say, Case."

"That's why I'm here, bro."

Casey was my shaggy-haired best friend, a redhead with freckles and a raspy voice. He wasn't big, but he was strong. He played eighth-grade football with the hunt-and-kill mind of a Cro-Magnon, and I felt sorry for anyone who had to face him.

I took off my glasses. For this trip I'd tied nylon fishing line to the stems and made a cord so that if my glasses fell off I wouldn't lose them. Without them everything looked blurry.

"Where's your dad?" I asked, rubbing my eyes.

"Making coffee." Casey picked up his mess kit and checked to see if everything was in it.

My dad was a few thousand miles away. He was supposed to be flying in tomorrow or the next day from a job that had ended in Alaska. He was a big-ship skipper and took freighters all across the world, which meant he was away a lot. But when he was home he was on me like a four-star general. We got along okay, I guess, but it took him a few

2

days to get out of his big-boat-boss mode. He wasn't a fan of my spending time with the Scout troop because he wanted me home helping Mom while he was away. But I liked Scouts, and was learning good things, and I wanted him to be proud of that.

"Hey, Dylan," Casey said. "We're packing the van, remember?"

I blinked and put my glasses back on. "Yeah, sorry."

"So," Casey said, his hair sprouting up like a pineapple top. "Take both our tents or share one?"

"Why take two?"

"Yeah. Mine's bigger."

"Yours, then. Hey . . . you need to rake that weed patch on your head."

He grinned and pulled his camo boonie hat out of his back pocket and slapped it on. "That help?"

"Not really. Ugly is ugly, ah?"

Casey threw his mess kit at me. I ducked. "Watch your back while you sleeping, punk," he said. "Anyway, you just jealous 'cause I got the ladies'-man hair, right? They like red, you know, not that rotten-banana color you got."

I laughed. "That's good, that's good."

"We aim to please."

He tugged his boonie hat closer to his head. It used to belong to his dad, a former U.S. marine. "*Still* a marine," Mr. Bellows always corrected us. "Once a marine, always a marine, and don't you forget it." Casey wore that hat everywhere—school, Scouts, church, even to my cousin's wedding, though my mom snatched it off his head and stuffed it into her purse.

3

Casey was going to be a marine, too. "Special Operations," he said. "Only real men survive." I'd known Casey all my life and knew he could do it.

We piled our gear in the middle of the van, leaving room to sit around the edges.

"Help me with the quartermaster box," Casey said, heading into the garage. "Weighs a ton." The box was the size of a giant cooler and held our big cookstove, lanterns, cooking gear, first-aid kit, ropes, knives, U.S. Army foldable shovels, and other tools. "Grab that end."

"Stand down, shrimp," I said. "I'll carry it by myself."

"Be my guest."

It was heavy, but I was taller than Casey and I could get my arms around it better than he could. I was used to lifting because we were working out with a weight set in my garage, trying to bulk up for high school football. But we were only eighth graders and still had a long way to go.

I lugged the box to the van and shoved it in, wondering how we'd fit into that shoe box on wheels with all the gear we had. There'd be eight Scouts, two adult leaders, and a driver.

We waited in the yard for Mr. Bellows, who was our scoutmaster. Casey dropped to the grass and started doing push-ups, grunting. "Five, six, seven—"

"What's taking your dad so long?"

"Coffee . . . nine, ten . . . gotta have it. You know . . . cops." Mr. Bellows was a Hilo Police Department detective.

Casey fell to the grass.

"How many?" I said.

"Twenty. . . . Usually do fifty . . . every morning."

"You're an animal."

4

"Thank you."

Mr. Bellows opened the door from the kitchen and ducked into the garage. He eased the door shut and winked. "Don't want to wake the boss."

"No, sir, we sure don't," Casey said. He stood and slapped bits of grass and dirt off his hands.

Mr. Bellows often referred to Mrs. Bellows as the boss, as though she ruled the house and if we woke her she'd come out with a stick. But I knew he was kidding. She was one of the nicest people I'd ever met, and always treated me like her own son. Mr. Bellows did, too.

Mr. Bellows still looked like a marine, clean, lean, and fit as a boot-camp drill sergeant. He measured six foot one the day all of us in the troop marked our height on the wall in Casey's garage. He had red hair like Casey, but his was whitewalled, military style. On the inside of his right forearm was a four-inch tattoo: *Semper Fidelis*. "Got that before I got my brain," he'd said. "But I like what it says, Always Faithful."

He raised his coffee cup and silver thermos. "I'm a whole man now. You boys ready?"

"Just waiting for you, old man," Casey said.

Mr. Bellows grunted and glanced around, saw that we'd packed everything. "Excellent. Let's roll!"

2
THE JUNGLE

Casey rode up front with his dad. I sat in the back, leaning against my pack, loving the freedom of being out on the road, getting away. I wanted Dad to come places with us, too, wanted to do things together. But when he got back from his weeks or months at sea, he liked to stay home with me, mom, and my sixteen-year-old sister, Dana. I guess I couldn't blame him.

Mr. Bellows hummed as he drove.

"Who we picking up first?" Casey asked.

"Sam . . . then Zach, Tad, Mike and his dad, Billy and his brother, who's going to drive this beast home. After that we grab Louie and head out."

I stretched my legs out, for a moment wishing I was back home asleep like Dana. Mom would be getting up at dawn to pad outside in her jammie bottoms and T-shirt to pick the newspaper out of the bushes. But Dana would sleep till noon.

The tires hummed on the highway. I closed my eyes.

I was jolted awake when someone opened the side door and tossed a backpack in.

"Morning, Sam," Mr. Bellows said. "You ready?"

"Yes, sir, Mr. Bellows."

"Climb aboard."

Sam jumped in, shut the door, and found a spot across from me. We nodded. Sam was eleven and the smallest kid in the troop. He was half Chinese, half French, and as tough as his spiky black hair made him look. "You awake?" I asked.

"Yep."

Next stop, the headlights washed over Zach, waiting out on the street holding his boots. No lights on in his house. He climbed in and sat next to Sam. Zach was twelve, skinny, and in my opinion, short on common sense. I flicked my eyebrows to say, hey. He smiled.

At Tad's, Casey had to go knock on the door. Tad's mom ushered Tad out with a kiss on the top of his head. She waved at Mr. Bellows. "Be careful."

Mr. Bellows raised a finger off the wheel, nodding.

Tad bumbled out to the van, a dreamy kid. I scooted over to make room. His hair was wet and he smelled of soap. Like Sam, he was eleven, and new to the troop. The young guys started talking. I closed my eyes and leaned my head back. They yapped like mynah birds.

At Mike Paia's house, Casey jumped in back so Mike's dad could sit up front. Reverend Paia was a Methodist minister and our assistant scoutmaster. I liked the Reverend. He was kind of pudgy and always happy. Mike would look just like him when he was older.

Mike settled in, mumbling hello. He had curly black hair. He was fifteen and getting flabby because he liked lying around on the beach. He wasn't into sports. He rubbed his hands together.

"Cold?" I said.

"Revved up. Aren't you?"

I shrugged. "Sure." We were going to the most remote spot on the island. It would be like going to Mars. "This trip will be awesome."

"And then some."

"Argh," Tad spat, trying to lace up his boots.

"Here," I said. "Give me one."

He put both feet in my lap. I tightened the laces and double-knotted them. "Too tight?"

He shook his head. "Thanks."

"No problem."

Billy Wheeler and his older brother, Jesse, got in next. Billy was eleven. He wore a silver chain around his neck, and in Scout meetings he sat running it across his lips. He was jumpy, and you could always get a shriek out of him if you came up from behind and said *boo!*

"Thanks for driving the van back, Jesse," Mr. Bellows said.

"Hey, I got to wake Billy up with an ice cube . . . already it's a great day."

"I'll get him back," Billy said.

Jesse scoffed. "In your dreams."

I smiled.

We headed back out to the road. In the east, dawn was barely beginning to show.

Twenty minutes later we turned onto a rough dirt road that led into a jungle. The van jerked over ruts and small rain-washed ravines, the headlights bouncing in the bushes. Glimpses of light squinted from dark, sagging houses lurking in the trees.

We fell silent.

I leaned toward Casey. "Louie lives *here*?"

"Coming up."

The van lurched over the ruts, camping gear sliding around in the van. Abandoned refrigerators and moldy couches swallowed by weeds and vines sat in every other yard. I'd never even thought about where Louie lived. He'd just joined; he showed up at the meetings and disappeared afterwards. "You been here before?"

"Once, with Dad."

"Why?"

"Shhh."

A faded turquoise four-door Ford Fairlane sat rusting in Louie's yard. Casey leaned close so the others wouldn't hear. "Louie sleeps in that car sometimes."

"How do you know?"

"Trust me."

I nodded. It was Casey's dad's job to know about people in his district. I studied the car. Its back window was shattered and looked like a giant spiderweb.

"You know he has an older brother?" Casey said.

"No."

"Arrested three times. Shoplifting, fighting, and racing."

"Racing?"

"Cars. Street racing, at night."

"Wild."

Mr. Bellows pulled into Louie's yard.

Three huge dogs charged out from under the porch, showing teeth and barking with deep-throated sucking sounds. Reverend Paia rolled up his window.

The headlights lit the front of the once-white house. Louie was sitting on the steps with his gear in the weeds at his feet.

The dogs leaped at the windows of the van, their claws clicking and scratching the doors. A light went on in the house next door. Those dogs would wake the whole neighborhood if Louie didn't shut them up.

Louie stood and swung his pack over his shoulder, squinting into the headlights. He flicked long strands of black hair out of his eyes as he came toward us. He was mostly Hawaiian and Filipino. On the wall in Casey's garage he measured six foot one, three inches taller than me, and he was all muscle. He wore baggy shorts and a loose black T-shirt with the sleeves cut off. He was the same age as Mike, fifteen, but he sure looked older. Like a man, ten years too soon. I couldn't take my eyes off him.

"Hush," Louie whispered to the dogs. They whimpered and slunk back into the black gap beneath the porch.

Reverend Paia rolled his window down and Casey pushed the van door open. The racket of the younger guys spilled out into the night.

When they saw Louie, they shut up.

3
VOLCANO

Louie tossed his gear onto the pile in the middle of the van. He nodded to Mr. Bellows and climbed in. Jesse moved to our side to make room.

"Hey," Mike said. He tapped the space next to him for Louie.

"Hey."

The van lurched when Louie sat. He flicked his eyebrows at Jesse to thank him for moving over. Jesse gave him a thumbs-up.

Instead of boots, Louie wore old running shoes with no socks. I didn't think they'd last the weekend, not where we were going. He sat with his knees up, his arms resting on them. Around his neck he wore a leather cord with a shark's tooth and a silver skull hanging from it. A thin white scar slashed across his upper lip.

I looked away when he caught me watching him.

Mr. Bellows swung the van around and jerked up the rutted dirt road. "You ready for this, Louie?"

"Sure," Louie mumbled, resting his head back against the van.

Louie had come into the troop with a chip on his shoulder the size of Australia. Every time he looked at you, there was always the hint of spit in his eyes. He acted like we were flies, something to be batted away. Except for Mike, who was part Hawaiian like Louie, which in Louie's mind made Mike okay.

But I was not okay.

Because there was something personal between us, something that nobody but us knew about.

When Louie first showed up at a troop meeting, we were squatting around Mike, doing lashings in Casey's garage. Mr. Bellows was late, and Mike was trying to show us how to rope logs together to make a raft.

When Mr. Bellows drove up, we all turned to look. There was someone with him, a new kid. I remember actually feeling my jaw drop. All thoughts of the raft vanished. It's *him*, I thought. I stood, my hands already beginning to sweat.

The new guy thumped the door shut and glanced around the yard. He wore loose camo shorts and a black T-shirt, with rubber slippers and long black hair that he flicked out of his eyes.

He'd changed. His scrawny arms had fattened with muscle. His jaw was square. He took us in with hooded eyes.

It had been over two years since I'd run into him. I blinked, the memory flooding back.

Mr. Bellows put a hand on his back and motioned toward the garage. They came toward us. I almost stopped breathing, remembering every little detail of those five minutes when our lives had crossed.

It was an accident. Or my bad luck.

It was near the end of fifth grade, almost summer. I was heading home from school on my bike, cutting across the middle school baseball field. Taking my time, daydreaming. My head snapped up when I heard a shout, and then a yelp. I turned toward the dugout. My front tire hit a rut in the dry grass and I fell off my bike.

"Gimme it!" someone shouted.

I struggled up, my bike lying at my feet. Some big high school guy had a kid who looked like a seventh or eighth grader by his shirt and was slapping him around, ripping into the kid's pocket for something, shouting, "Where is it!"

But the kid kept his mouth shut, taking the beating.

The big guy looked up and saw me gawking.

I stood frozen as he turned back and went through the kid's pockets. He found what he was looking for. Not money, something else. He jammed it into his own pocket and shoved the kid down. Then he headed toward me.

I scrambled to pick up my bike, so scared I fell and got tangled up in the bike frame. The big guy was suddenly there, his foot on the front tire. He looked down, grinning. "You scared, haole?" he said.

I crawled away backwards, nodding.

"You should be." He laughed and walked away.

13

My heart pounded. I glanced over at the dugout. The kid staggered up, and our eyes met. He brushed himself off, his face contorted with hate and shame. Getting beat up was one thing. Having someone younger than him see it was another. The look on his face said he wanted to kill me, kill anyone. He started running toward me.

I jerked my bike up and got on, started pedaling, wobbly at first, then picking up speed. I could hear his feet thumping on the hard dirt behind me. But he couldn't keep up with the bike. When he finally gave up he yelled, "I'll get you!"

I never took that way home again.

Luckily, my parents sent me to a private school the next year, out of that district. But I knew that kid would never forget me . . . and I wouldn't forget him.

Now he was heading into the garage with Mr. Bellows.

"Boys, I'd like you to meet Louie Domingo," Mr. Bellows said. "He's thinking about joining the troop."

Louie said nothing. Bored eyes.

Everyone mumbled hello.

I squatted back down. Maybe he won't remember me.

"So," Mr. Bellows said. "What are we doing here, Mike?" Mike was our senior patrol leader.

"Lashings."

"Keep going, then." Mr. Bellows knelt to watch. "Sit, Louie."

Louie squatted on his heels with his arms crossed over his knees. His blank expression said: What am I doing here with these dorks in stupid uniforms?

I tried to catch Casey's eye. What was his dad thinking?

14

I scrunched lower, half hidden behind Casey.

Louie hadn't noticed me, or if he had, he was keeping it to himself. My old fear swelled in my gut. Even so, it was impossible not to sneak glances at him. His eyes were the color of copper, unusual for a guy as dark as he was. They gave him a kind of power, like magnets, sucking you in.

Slowly, those eyes turned my way.

He stared at me. I thought I saw a small grin.

I looked down.

Mike said, "Dylan, your turn."

I looked up. "Huh?"

"Your turn to lash."

"Yeah, sure." I moved closer. Picked up the rope. My fingers felt clumsy and I couldn't get it right.

"Start over," Mr. Bellows said. "See it in your mind before you go through the moves."

I nodded.

Starting over didn't help. My mind wasn't anywhere near where it needed to be.

"I can do it," Louie said, so softly I barely heard.

Everyone turned.

Mr. Bellows tipped his head toward Louie. I tossed Louie the rope without looking at him.

Still squatting, he re-coiled it. Slowly, taking his time. I looked at his hands, not his face. He duckwalked closer to the logs. In a matter of seconds he lashed them together, tight and perfect, then sat back on his heels and gazed at a spot of oil on the garage floor.

15

"Wow," Mike said.

Mr. Bellows grinned. "Where'd you learn that, Louie?"

"My uncle has a boat."

"He taught you well," Mr. Bellows said. "So why don't you take over and teach the rest of us how to do it?"

Without a word Louie untied his work and showed us the easy, smooth steps you go through to lash logs together.

Mr. Bellows winked at me.

I nodded and whispered, "He's good."

The van rattled and squeaked as we headed back down the dirt road from Louie's house to the highway.

Mr. Bellows glanced over his shoulder. "Glad you could get off work to join us, Louie."

Louie said nothing, his head back, bouncing with the van. He worked weekends at a drive-in called Jimmy's Place, not too far from his house. Mike said that Louie had told the owner he was sixteen and old enough to work. But the owner didn't care how old he was as long as he showed up on time. He paid Louie in cash, less than minimum wage. Louie was the only one of us who had a job. This was the first time he'd gone anywhere with the troop.

The young guys stayed quiet.

Louie stared at me. I squeezed my hands into fists and looked away. If he still wanted to kill me, he would have done it by now.

He kept staring. Maybe I was wrong.

"Settle in, men," Mr. Bellows said when we got to the smooth paved highway. "We'll be at the trailhead in no time."

The steady whine of the tires made my eyelids droop. I dozed off and woke up twenty miles later.

The sky by then had turned a soft purple-gray, the bubble of dawn glowing in the east. The young guys started talking again, getting excited about the idea of hiking down the cliffs below the volcano to camp in a sandy cove at the edge of the sea.

Across from me, Louie and Mike slept. Casey was oiling his pocketknife. I smiled when I noticed the corner of a small blue blanket sticking out of Tad's backpack. I remembered my own blanket—what was left of it, anyway—now stored in a plastic bag in the garage. Dad made Mom steal it away from me. Funny how you get attached to certain things.

Zach's backpack looked like it had been packed by a chimpanzee. Sam's was brand-new, not a dusty mark on it, stuffed to the limit. His mother had probably packed it for him. I winced, thinking about how heavy it must be for a little kid. But Sam wasn't a complainer. He'd carry it no matter how much it weighed.

Louie's gear was minimal, a battered sports bag with a shoulder strap. He had no tent, but Mike did. "Who needs a tent?" Louie'd snapped when we were planning this trip. "Sleep under the stars like the old-timers."

"What old-timers?" I'd asked. I'd thought it was an

innocent question. But thinking back, I changed my mind. It was cocky, and I didn't know why I'd said it.

He'd studied me with narrowed eyes and said, "Guys who came here before you, haole." *Haole* came out with a threat nailed to it. It was a word that could mean many things: white guy or white punk, or it could say, I like you, white punk, or sometimes, You dead meat, white punk. It was one of those words you had to take with the rest of what was going on around it. This time it wasn't the I-like-you version. Heat had rushed to my face.

Now Louie opened his eyes and shifted to stretch his legs. Sam scurried to give him more room. Louie nodded, then looked across at me, blank-eyed.

I stared back.

He didn't blink.

I didn't blink.

Casey elbowed me.

I bunched my lips and turned away. Louie could tie good knots, sure, but maybe an ape could, too, if you taught it.

A while later, Mr. Bellows pointed and said something to Reverend Paia. I stretched to see out the front window as the van slowed and turned onto a narrow road. The sun splashed light onto the windshield as we drove through the jungle.

"Where are we?" I asked.

"Heading to the trailhead," Reverend Paia said. "Just turned onto Chain of Craters Road."

When I sat back, Louie was still watching me.

"What?" I said.

He didn't answer, his eyes blank. He'd never brought up that day in the dugout.

But I knew he remembered.

And he knew I did, too.

4
HILINA PALI

We broke out of the trees and turned down an even narrower road that rolled out over a wide expanse of scrub brush. The road ended at a bluff.

Reverend Paia turned in his seat and smiled. "End of the line, boys."

We piled out and stretched. There was nothing there. No people, no buildings, no anything for as far as I could see. I felt like a cat dumped in the wilderness.

We were high up on the flank of Mauna Loa, the long, sloping mountain volcano, and looking down from the cliff, you could see the ocean far below, stretching out to vanish over the horizon. A round geological benchmark said we were 2,282 feet above sea level.

Another sign read: *Hilina Pali—formed by the downward*

movement of great sections of the mountainside. The result-ing cliff, or fault scarp, is 1,500 feet high and 12 miles long.

The downward movement of the mountainside.

"Yow," I whispered. "You read this, Case?"

"Long way down."

Behind him Louie stood with his arms crossed and his head cocked, like, Show me something I don't know. But I could see his eyes scanning the landscape.

"Let's get the gear out so Jesse can go home," Reverend Paia said.

"I'd rather be going with you," Jesse said, "but . . . gotta work, ah?"

"Maybe next time."

"So where exactly am I picking you up?"

Mr. Bellows pulled out a folded piece of paper. "I drew you a map. It's down on the road to Kalapana."

"Hoo, that's a long walk out."

"Still wish you were going with us?"

Jesse smiled. "Maybe not." He turned to help unload.

Reverend Paia rummaged around in the quartermaster box and took out the first-aid kit and a few cooking utensils. "Leave the box in the van," he said.

"Okay, gather your gear, men," Mr. Bellows said.

Jesse started the van, waved, and headed back up the nar-row ribbon of road. Next time we saw him it would be Sun-day, three days from now. And we'd be miles away from here.

A movement in the distance caught my eye. I blocked the sun with my hand and squinted. Something was slinking through the weeds and scrub grass along the ridge of the escarpment about a quarter mile off. The weeds broke, and for a moment I could see them clearly. They were thin and scraggy.

Dogs?

Out here?

There were two. One big and dark, the other smaller, and white. They moved like ghosts, smooth, and low to the ground. Neither one of them glanced over at us, as if they wanted only to escape from view.

"Casey, you bring your binoculars?"

"Sure." He dug into his backpack.

"What do you see?" Mike said.

"Dogs."

Casey looked up, still feeling for his binoculars. Louie and Mike scanned the landscape. "I don't see anything," Mike said.

I pointed. "Out there. See them in the grass?"

Casey found his binoculars and raised them to his eyes. Louie grabbed them out of his hand.

"Hey!" Casey said.

Louie blocked Casey with his shoulder as he focused the lenses. Casey made a grab to get the binoculars back. Louie raised them over his head.

"Give them back, Louie," Mike said.

Louie gave Mike a snarly look. Mike backed off, shaking his head.

"Dylan!" Mr. Bellows called. "Get your troop together. We got some miles to hike."

"Yes, sir, Mr. Bellows," I said.

In Scouts there's a position called senior patrol leader,

which you get by the vote of your fellow Scouts. This year, I'd won that vote and had taken the job from Mike. Mike was happy to hand it over. It was a lot of work. When I told Dad I was the new SPL, he put his hand on my shoulder and said, "Now you're speaking my language."

"All right, guys," I said, "form a line."

Louie grinned and tossed the binoculars to Casey. "Catch."

Casey caught them and scowled at Louie.

Louie flicked his eyebrows.

Was this how it was going to be?

I frowned but kept my mouth shut.

Mr. Bellows stood looking back at us, his eyes shaded by a blue L.A. Dodgers baseball cap. The top of his backpack was so loaded with gear it stuck up higher than his head. "We have a problem back there?"

"No, sir," I said.

Mr. Bellows shook his head and sighed. "Come on, boys, we've got to get down to the coast before it gets too hot."

"Too hot already," I mumbled.

Louie leaned into my ear and whispered, "Hey, Senior Patrol Loser, you can't take the heat or what?"

Whoa! I moved away from him. "You really got a problem, you know, Louie?"

"I ain't got no problem, punk. But you might." He grinned, a sight I was coming to hate.

Reverend Paia heard and moved around behind us. "Think I'll take up the rear. Don't want to lose anyone."

Louie winked at me. I turned and spat. Why would Mr.

Bellows go out of his way to pollute our troop with a creep like this? Didn't make sense.

"Shoulder up!" I called, and struggled to get my arms through the straps of my pack. How much Louie Domingo trouble waited for me down where we were going?

Forget it, I thought. Don't let him ruin the trip. I took a deep breath. Mr. Bellows waved us forward.

We started down Hilina Pali Trail, Mr. Bellows taking the lead. The young guys followed him, then Casey, me, Louie, Mike, and Reverend Paia.

My backpack felt like a fifty-pound bag of dog pellets. Casey and I were cooking breakfast on Sunday, so along with everything else, I had canned peaches and oatmeal. Casey had bacon in a cold pack.

I glanced over the edge of the scarp, a two-thousand-foot sloping drop to the sea. Down there somewhere was a campground called Halape, our destination. "There's a coconut grove, and a few park shelters to sleep in," Mr. Bellows had told us. "Fishermen go there, sort of a secret spot."

But all I could see now was an endless shoreline of black lava. "Man, that's grim."

Casey laughed. "It gets better."

I glanced past Louie and Mike at Mauna Loa, the island's most active volcano. Its rounded purple peak stood cloudless in the far distance. It looked peaceful, asleep.

I turned back, already sweating. There was no wind. The earth smelled like rust. My neck and arms were starting to burn, the sun pouring down like molten stone. The blue ocean far below looked better by the minute.

Dust puffed around our boots as we slipped on the loose

pebbles on the steep trail. I thought about how weird it was to see dogs way out here, where there was nothing but rocks and weeds. How did they live?

"Watch your step," Mr. Bellows said. "We don't want anyone going over the edge."

"This is the easy part." Casey nodded toward the long, empty coast far below. "Wait till we hike out over all that lava. It'll eat your boots like a stump grinder."

I knew what he meant. There were two kinds of lava: *pahoehoe* and *a'a*. Pahoehoe flowed like mud and dried in smooth rolls, and that was the kind you always wanted to run into. A'a was the opposite. It sputtered as it flowed, and dried quickly in sharp and jagged spikes. Hiking over it wouldn't be easy.

"Let's make a deal, Case," I said. "You keep your good news to yourself and I won't push you over the cliff."

"Hey, don't shoot the messenger."

I turned to look back at where I'd spotted the dogs. Empty scrub brush shimmered in the heat.

5
STEEP SLOPE TO NOWHERE

We crept down the trail in silence. The face of the fault rose straight up on our left. On our right, a deep precipice fell to a long slide of jagged rocks. I hugged the left side.

A moment later, Sam slipped and nearly fell over the edge. Billy grabbed his pack and hung on. Casey grabbed them both.

Mr. Bellows raised his hand for us to stop. "You okay, Sam?"

"Yes, sir, I . . . My foot just slipped."

"Listen up," Mr. Bellows said to all of us. "This trail isn't in the best shape. Watch out for loose rock. If you fall, you're going to be in a world of trouble."

I glanced down the slope. It made me dizzy.

"You ready, Sam?" Mr. Bellows said.

"Yes, sir," Sam answered, in the way Mr. Bellows liked. Respect was something he pounded into us. Respect for nature, your elders, your country, your team, your parents, yourself, and each other, and nothing said respect better than *sir.*

We continued down the trail, boots grinding on loose rock. Beads of sweat rolled down the side of my face. "What'd I tell you about the heat?" Casey said.

"I'm a believer."

Casey was the only one of us who'd been to Halape. Because his dad was the scoutmaster, Casey'd gone along on his older brother Jack's campout a while back. Jack had just flown off to college in California. I carried the American flag at his Eagle Court of Honor before he left. Scouting was a big deal in the Bellows family. Mr. Bellows was an Eagle, his brother in Honolulu was an Eagle, and now Jack, and for sure Casey would be one, too.

And me.

It would take a lot of work and commitment, but I'd be right there with Casey, whether Dad was part of it or not. It would be mine alone.

Our troop was lucky, because Mr. Bellows and Reverend Paia cared. They worked hard for us, kept us pumped up about working on advancement and merit badges, never let us slack off. They celebrated when we succeeded and helped us when we didn't.

The second time Louie came to a meeting, Mr. Bellows had said to us, "One day you'll look back on your Scout experience and be proud of what you did. I know you get teased for it at school, but that's a good thing, if you think

27

about it. You're learning how to stand up to crowd mentality. You're learning how to think and act for yourselves. Sometimes that takes courage. I'm proud of you boys." I'd expected Louie to smirk, like, What *dorks*! But he'd listened . . . still with that bored look, but he'd listened.

Now, heading down to Halape, I was jolted out of my thoughts when Louie grabbed my backpack and nearly knocked me off the trail. "Hey!"

"Stand still. Your sleeping bag is coming loose."

He secured it in three quick motions.

"Uh . . . thanks."

"Move on."

❖ ❖ ❖

After a few steep miles the trail leveled out. The dangerous part was behind us. From here on it would be an easy slope to the sea.

"Rest a few minutes," Mr. Bellows said. He dropped his pack and sat on a rock in the dusty weeds.

I shrugged mine off, too, and pulled my sweaty T-shirt away from my skin, shaking it with my fingers. "What I'd like right now is to sit in the ocean."

Casey fanned his face with his boonie hat. "You need one of these. Your head's going to fry."

"Tell me."

We sat in the dirt.

Up front, Mr. Bellows took a long draw from his canteen. Reverend Paia walked past us to join him. They spoke in low voices.

I leaned back on my pack. "How can anything grow here? Must rain about once every five years, if at all."

Casey took out his canteen. "It rains."

A pebble hit the dirt not far from my boots.

I looked up. Louie flicked his eyebrows. He and Mike were sitting in the weeds, off by themselves.

"Ignore him," Casey whispered.

"Sure, and I'll just ignore it when a scorpion crawls up my leg, too."

Casey snickered.

"You know, Case, what I can't figure is why your dad brought him into our troop."

Casey shrugged.

I took out my canteen and drank. The water was still cool. I felt like drinking the whole thing.

"Better ration that," Casey said. "No fresh water at Halape."

"What are we supposed to drink when we run out? Seawater?"

"Stink water."

"What?"

"You'll see."

I looked at my canteen, wanting another long drink. I screwed the cap back on. Dust had gathered on my glasses. I took them off and rubbed the lenses with my T-shirt, then let them hang around my neck on the fishing line.

I dug into my backpack for my towel and draped it over my head for shade. I closed my eyes.

We sat, motionless, like lizards.

Where were those dogs now? What did they eat? Birds?

Grass? Mongooses? Or did they go begging for scraps at the Volcano House Hotel up by the crater?

"Did you know Louie's dad was a marine?" Casey said, low.

I lifted the towel and peeked out. "Maybe I should join up."

Casey shook his head. "Naah, you too soft. They wouldn't take you."

I bunched my fist. "Maybe not, but I can take you."

Casey laughed. I dropped the towel back over my face.

"This place we're going," he said. "You'll like it. Wait till you see the crack."

I pulled the towel off my head. "The crack?"

"A swimming hole in this huge underground cavern surrounded by solid rock. The water's cool in the day and warm at night."

"I'm ready."

"It'll make all this hiking worth it."

"That'd be good."

To tell the truth, I'd rather have been home hiking up to a tall glass of ice water.

Another pebble hit close and rolled up to my boot. I whipped around. Mike, sitting with Louie, had his head down, laughing.

"Missed," Louie called. "I was trying for hit that stick by your foot."

I picked up the stick and flung it farther away.

"Dad," Casey called. "We're getting stiff. We gotta move."

Mr. Bellows nodded and grunted up, hefted his monster

pack onto his shoulders. Reverend Paia headed back to the end of the line, tapping Mike's shoulder as he passed.

We all groaned and creaked up.

An hour later we headed around the last hill, and there it was.

Halape.

"Wow," I whispered. A thick green coconut grove curved around a white-sand beach. And beyond, a sky blue ocean sat smooth and calm.

Casey pointed over to a deep fissure in the rocks to our right. "The crack," he said. He and I jumped the rocks to look down into it. The water was emerald green, winking in the sun. I looked up. This place was a paradise, a small fraction of the old island that had somehow been spared by the massive lava flows that had turned the rest of the coastline into a desolate wasteland.

"Senior patrol leader," Mr. Bellows said, "take us in."

I dipped my head and led the troop down to the sea.

6
STINGING ANTS AND STINK WATER

Casey and I dropped our packs and ran to the beach. "Look at this place," I said. Halape was untouched, a land in a time before man.

"Nice, huh?"

"Incredible."

Casey lifted his chin toward his dad. "He can forget about crime down here. Not many places he can do that."

I nodded. "He's got a tough job."

"Yeah, but he likes it."

"I could live here."

What made Halape so amazing was the fact that it was there at all. It was like an ice cube in the desert, because everywhere else along that coastline there was only hardened black lava and a few scrubby weeds. I looked in both directions, trying to imagine what it looked like before the volcanoes blew and covered it up.

Slow waves rolled in and ran up onto the white sand. Low green patches of *naupaka* bushes and a few tangled *hau* trees lined its edge, separating the cove from the rocky inlands. Nearby, the shady grove of coconut trees shimmered in the sun. *You got to come see this place, Dad. Just once. After that, you'll beg me to take you every place we go.*

I wish.

I turned and looked back at the land sweeping up to Casey's swimming hole and beyond to the thousand-foot cliff that loomed over Halape. "It's called Pu'u Kapukapu," Casey'd said. "Means regal hill."

It was regal, all right, but it was way more than a hill. It was a flat-faced cliff with huge boulders pocking it. We'd be camping right below it.

Reverend Paia gazed out to sea, his hands on his hips. "What an inspiration."

"I knew you'd like it," Mr. Bellows said.

What was inspiring to me was the thought of getting my boots off and my feet in the ocean.

We headed single file into the coconut grove. A slight breeze cooled my face as sunbursts on the ocean blinked under the waggling palm fronds. Mr. Bellows spread his arms wide. "Pick a spot."

Beyond the coconut grove were a couple of three-sided park shelters, an old cabin, and an outhouse just uphill. But it was the ocean that whispered to me. A small island sat just offshore. We could easily swim out and explore it. "Can we go swimming, Mr. Bellows?"

"Sure, Dylan. But after we get set up."

"That water is calling my name."

"Mine, too, but you need to know that there's a pretty strong current out there beyond the island. You can't see it, but believe me, it's there. You get caught in that and we'll have to fly down to Tahiti to pick you up. Listen, all of you. Do not—I repeat, do *not*—swim past the island. Is that clear?"

We all nodded.

"Forget the ocean," Casey said, stuffing his boonie hat in his back pocket. "We got the crack!"

"That you do." Mr. Bellows rubbed the mop of hair on Casey's head. "But first let's set up camp. Dylan, you got your lunch crew in place?"

"Yes, sir."

"Good." He turned to the rest of the guys. "Before you pitch your tents, your SPL will assign buddies, and remember, never go *anywhere* without your buddy."

"Yes, sir," we all said.

Mr. Bellows tapped my shoulder. "All yours." He left to set up his tent.

"Okay," I said. "Buddies—me and Casey, Louie and Mike, Tad and Zach, Sam and Billy. That okay?"

Louie smirked. Everyone else nodded.

I waited to see if Louie agreed. I couldn't tell. "Louie?"

He turned and spat. "No problem."

He and Mike headed down the coast toward the point, where the cliff came closer to the sea. Sam, Billy, and Tad decided to set their tents up in the coconut grove near Mr. Bellows and Reverend Paia.

That left me, Casey, and Zach.

34

Zach was twelve, younger than me and Casey, but he wanted to hang around with us. Casey was just fine with that, because he liked Zach's sister, Sarah.

"Where you guys want to set up?" Zach said.

I shrugged. "You should prob'ly set up by Tad."

"Why? Buddies don't have to camp together, do they?"

"I guess not," I said. "You don't like him, or what?"

"He's okay. It's just that . . . those three . . . they get kind of—"

"Weird?" Casey said.

"Yeah."

Silly was the word my mom would have used. Always goofing off.

"So where we setting up?" Casey said.

I glanced around, wanting to stay away from Louie and Mike. "How about there?" I said, pointing my chin toward one of the park shelters. "Save us having to set up the tent."

"Looks good to me."

"Me too," Zach said.

"You have to put up a tent," Casey said. "Part of your Second Class requirements, remember? Sleep in a tent you pitch?"

Zach sagged. "Oh . . . right."

Casey winked at me. "We get the hotel."

Zach dropped his gear on the sand. Casey and I went into the shelter. We'd passed the tent requirement a long time ago. We were Star Scouts now, working up to Life, the last level before Eagle. Mike was a Star, too. Louie wasn't even a Scout yet, as far as I knew.

The shelter was about halfway between the coconut

grove and the spot down the coast that Louie and Mike had chosen, which was a sandy nook enclosed within the arms of a rock outcropping. They were setting up Mike's tent. It had a flap that came out like a small awning in front. Nice spot— if the tide didn't come up in the night.

"What are you smiling about?" Casey said.

"You think it's high or low tide right now?"

Casey checked the beach. "I'd say it's low. See the junk up there on the sand? That's your high-water mark."

I glanced back at Louie and Mike's campsite.

"Nah," Casey said. "They're not that dumb."

I grinned. "Too bad."

Our hotel was a dirt-floored shelter with a slanted corrugated iron roof that drained rainwater into a catchment tank on the backside. "That's where you get your water," Casey said. "Go check it out."

I went around back to the tank and cupped some water in my hand. I raised it to my lips and spat. It smelled like a swamp. "Haw! We supposed to drink *that*?"

Casey staggered, laughing.

"Man, that's nasty!"

"You got to boil it first. Then it will taste good as lemonade."

"Impossible."

"You'll see."

The sides of the shelter were made of rocks held together by grainy concrete. In a good, solid wall the rocks are jigsawed together with no cement, like Hawaiians made them hundreds of years ago. Most of those old walls were still standing. But whoever had built this shelter hadn't taken that

36

kind of care. Chunks of cement fell away when I touched them.

I unrolled my thin rubber pad onto the dirt and puffed out my subzero sleeping bag on top of it. I hoped it wouldn't be too hot to sleep in. I sat down on it and took my glasses off to clean them. "What time you got?"

Casey checked his watch. "One-forty."

"No wonder I'm starving."

"Who's got lunch duty?"

"The young guys, who else?"

"That means what, peanut butter sandwiches?"

"Whatever it is, I'll eat it."

Casey chuckled.

"Yah!" I yelped, leaping up. I scrambled away from my sleeping bag, slapping at my legs. "Something bit me!"

Casey grabbed his sleeping bag and shook it. "Stinging ants!"

A line of them had set up a roadway through the shelter, and we'd set down right on top of them.

"We got to sleep with *these*?"

Casey used his T-shirt to slap the red ants out of the shelter. Then he dug out his bug repellent and sprayed a rectangle around his sleeping bag. "They won't cross over that."

He tossed me the spray and I painted a moat around my pad, thinking how funny it would be to see my sister, Dana, sleeping here. I could just see her slapping red ants out of her hair and shrieking her head off. She'd *hate* this place. So would Mom.

I tossed the bug spray back. "That ought to pucker their noses . . . if ants got noses."

"Now you only got the black widows to worry about," Casey said. "Oh, and the centipedes and flying roaches. Forgot about them."

"Thanks, Case, that was something I really wanted in my head."

"Anytime, bro."

"Zach," I called, rubbing my stinging shin. "You done setting up that tent? Time to go eat."

"Just waiting for you slackers."

Casey grinned. "Cocky, ah?"

I gazed out at the ocean—so blue, so close. Down the way, the coconut grove sat green against it, almost like a dream. It made me feel calm, like I could sit and stare at it for the rest of the day and not get bored. I humphed, thanking my lucky stars that Dad wasn't here. Probably take him two seconds to find something for me to be doing.

As we headed over to the main campsite in the coconut trees, I glanced up at Pu'u Kapukapu, the rocky cliff that loomed over us.

Relax. They wouldn't build these shelters under it if it was dangerous.

I heard voices and glanced back.

"Whatchoo looking?" Louie said, he and Mike following us to the coconut grove. I turned away.

A minute later a piece of driftwood spun past my ear, making me duck. Louie and Mike laughed.

"Hey!" I yelled, turning back with my fists balled. I'd had enough of this.

Casey grabbed me. "No, Dylan."

"He wants it."

"Don't."

Louie motioned me closer. Come on, punk. We go.

Casey jerked me around. "Forget it!"

Zach gaped, not knowing what to do.

I bunched my lips. Yeah, sure, forget it . . . until something hits me. Then me and him got a problem.

"It's not worth it," Casey added.

"Fine."

We walked on.

I didn't get Mike. Why didn't he step in? He used to be a good guy. It was Louie. He'd shamed Mike into turning against us, because Mike had some Hawaiian in him. "Where's your pride, man?" I'd once heard Louie say to Mike. Mike had no answer. I didn't think Louie wanted one.

"How'd he get that scar, anyway?" Zach whispered.

"Kissed a barracuda," I said, still steaming.

Casey humphed. "He fell off the roof of his house," he said, almost whispering. "His brother made him go up and get his stuck football."

I glanced at Casey. "And you know this because . . ."

"Dad . . . Louie told him."

"What else did he tell him?"

"Can't say."

I spat. "Right."

"Really, I can't," he whispered. "Dad doesn't want rumors going around."

"About Louie?"

"Uh-huh."

I grabbed Casey's arm and pulled him off the trail. Zach kept going toward camp. Louie and Mike passed, Louie's eyes drilling mine. When they'd gone by, he turned away, laughing. That was when I saw the knife. It was in a leather sheath, sticking out of his back pocket.

"Tell me," I said, still looking at the knife.

"Not now . . . later."

7
THE CRACK

"Way to go, little punks," Mike said, and slapped Billy, Sam, and Tad on the back. "That was a good lunch."

The rest of us nodded, still wolfing down oranges, bologna sandwiches with mustard on soft white bread, and small bags of Fritos that they'd packed in for our first meal. I could have eaten ten of everything.

Mr. Bellows and Reverend Paia sat off a ways, letting the guys working on advancing to Second Class manage the meal alone.

Louie belched and patted his stomach.

Mr. Bellows stood and pushed his blue Dodgers cap back on his head. "Listen up, men. The Reverend and I are going down the coast, see what's around the bend. Feel free to do some exploring, too . . . but don't drift too far."

Reverend Paia stood and put his straw hat back on, then grabbed a canteen. "Nobody goes off alone. You have buddies for a reason. Keep your eyes open and your common sense engaged." He pointed at me. "SPL . . . you're in charge."

I nodded. "Yes, sir."

Louie snickered.

"You can do whatever you like except go in the ocean," Mr. Bellows added. "For that you have to wait until we get back. Understood?"

Nods and mumbles, yeah.

Mr. Bellows turned to look out at the small island. "Last time, we spotted a shark just to the right of those rocks."

A shark?

They headed out, Mr. Bellows in his blue cap and Reverend Paia smiling under his floppy sun blocker.

"You heard it," I said. "Stay with your buddy."

"Me and Louie are going to check out the cliff," Mike said. "Just so you know."

Louie shoved him. "Why you talking to him, ah? You his slave?"

"Hey!"

"We go," Louie said.

When you get up to the cliff, jump off, I thought.

"I'm just telling him where we're going, that's all." They left.

Zach helped the young guys clean up the lunch mess. He had to stay with Tad anyway. "Make this place shine," I said.

Casey and I went down to the ocean, took off our boots,

and sat with our feet in the water. I closed my eyes. "Man, does that feel good!"

"Watch for eels," Casey said, and I jerked my feet back.

He laughed. "You are hopeless, bro, *hopeless.*"

I scowled, knowing he was right. I fell for everything. I skimmed a flat rock out into the bay. "You see that knife in Louie's pocket?"

"Yeah."

We sat for a moment in silence, the ocean calm, whispering.

"Bothers me," I said.

"Why?"

"Don't know."

"You don't have to worry about it."

"Because?"

"Because Dad knows what he's doing."

I let that thought sit a moment. It was answer enough. Mr. Bellows would never let Louie bring it if he didn't trust him. So he must trust him . . . but does he even know Louie has it?

I tossed another pebble into the water. Why am I thinking about this? I stuffed my socks into my boots and stood. "Your dad didn't say we couldn't swim in the crack, right?"

Casey looked up and raised an eyebrow. "You're right. Maybe you aren't so hopeless."

Five minutes later we were heading up to the crack in our swimming shorts, with rubber slippers slapping our feet and white towels hanging over our shoulders.

"You bring anything for sunburn?" I said.

"Oops."

I was glad I had my T-shirt on.

We stood at the top of the dirt trail that sloped down into the crack. It was dark down there, like somebody's old bomb shelter. But the water looked cool, and where the sun shined on it you could see shadows under every rock and pebble on the bottom. Farther in, the water ran back under the lava.

I looked up. No one in sight.

"What you looking for?"

"Mike and Louie."

"They won't tell," Casey said. "Anyway, Dad didn't say stay out of the crack, right? He just said don't go in the ocean."

"That's how I remember it, but maybe he meant don't go swimming at all."

"Then he would have said that."

"I guess."

We headed down the trail. Casey flipped off his rubber slippers, dropped his towel, and jumped. "Yeehaw!" he yelled coming up, his voice echoing through the cavernous crack.

I leaped in after him. The water was cool. It tasted slightly salty, but also fresh and earthy, like up in the rain forest. It was brackish, half springwater, half salt water seeping in from the sea. I dove under. "Hey!" I shouted as I popped back up. I wanted to hear my voice bounce around the rock walls. *Hey . . . hey,* it echoed.

The lip of the rocks that surrounded the crack above

framed the cloudless blue sky. It was like swimming in a well.

"All right, Case," I said, floating on my back. "This is about as private as it's going to get. Tell me about Louie."

Casey pulled himself up onto a ledge.

I climbed out and sat next to him, our feet in the water. "You know I'll keep my mouth shut."

"Okay, listen." He glanced once up the trail. "You got to *promise* to keep this to yourself. Dad only told me because I overheard him talking to Mom."

"Yeah, yeah, I promise. What did you hear?"

"See . . . Dad sort of . . . rescued him."

"From what?"

"One day Dad was snooping around an old abandoned warehouse . . . he was following up on leads he had on some guys who were stealing cars and dismantling them for parts."

"Louie was stealing cars?"

"No, no, not Louie. Dad just found him in that warehouse. . . . He was living there."

"Whoa," I said. "You mean using it like a fort. He lives in that house in the jungle, right?"

"Yeah, but when Dad found him, he was living in the warehouse. He ran away from home."

I whistled, low.

"So when Dad walked in—"

Casey stopped and looked up. A dark figure appeared, silhouetted against the blue sky at the top of the trail. I shaded my eyes.

45

Zach peered down on us, leaning forward with his hands on his knees. "How's the water?"

"Come on down," Casey shouted. "It's awesome!"

I frowned.

"Tell you more later," Casey said.

"Just tell me what your dad saw when he went into the warehouse."

"There was this room," Casey whispered. "The door was locked, but Dad jimmied it open. Inside, there was a bug-infested mattress on the floor, a box of clothes, a couple of cans of food, and a jug of water . . . and two schoolbooks."

"That's where Louie was living?"

"For more than a month. But get this—he was still going to school."

"You mean, from that warehouse? After running away?"

"That's what Dad said."

"Was he there when your dad went in?"

"No, but . . . Shhh."

"What are you guys whispering about?" Zach called across the water, pulling off his T-shirt.

"Secret," Casey said.

Zach tossed his shirt and shorts on the rocks and jumped in wearing only his boxers. He sank and came back up, water streaming from his face. "Ho, this is nice!" He swam over, pulled himself up on the ledge.

"Where's Tad?" I said, irritated. I wanted more of Casey's story. "You're supposed to be with him."

"With Billy and Sam. He didn't want to come up here."

"But, Zach," Casey said. "You're supposed to—"

"It's okay. He's with them."

I frowned and shook my head. "I hope you don't get caught." As SPL, I should have made him go back. But it wasn't easy bossing your friends around.

"He's *fine*," Zach said. "Those guys are just playing around, making dams in the tide pools."

Casey slipped off the shelf into the water.

I should have been worrying about Zach leaving his buddy, but I couldn't get that warehouse out of my head. If Louie ran away, wouldn't his parents assume he wasn't going to school? And if he wasn't going to school, wouldn't his parents wonder why they weren't getting a call about it? And wouldn't they call the school to find out why? If they did, they'd have found Louie.

This was too weird. I had to know more. "Zach, you really need to go find Tad."

Zach ignored me and dove off the shelf, swirling water following his feet down.

I looked up at the blue patch of sky. I could get more out of Casey tonight in the shelter.

But I couldn't wait that long.

When Zach came back up, I said, "You *need* to go get Tad, Zach. I mean it. What if he slips and falls and gets cut up on the rocks or something? You want to explain that to Casey's dad?"

Zach scowled. "All right . . . *jeese*. I'll go back and get him and drag him up here."

"We'll all go," Casey said. "All right, Dylan?"

No, not all right. I want more story. "Sure," I said with a sigh. "Why not."

We swam to the rocks and grabbed our towels, T-shirts,

47

and rubber slippers. Out in the sunlight it was so bright it felt like somebody'd stabbed a spear into my eyes. I hung my towel over my head.

We headed down to the tide pools.

No one was there.

8
LOST

"Look," Casey said, pointing down the coast.

Billy and Sam were squatting in the shallow water of a tide pool. All you could see was their heads.

"You see Tad?"

Casey hopped onto a large boulder and stretched as high as he could. "Just Billy and Sam."

I scowled at Zach.

"He was there when I left."

I tossed my towel and T-shirt down. We hurried toward Sam and Billy, jumping the rocks. I was grateful for the cushion of my rubber slippers, because in some places the lava was like sharks' teeth.

"Billy!" Casey called. "Sam!"

49

Their heads popped up.

"Where's Tad?" Zach said, breathless. He bent over and put his hands on his knees.

Sam glanced around. "He was here a minute ago."

I looked back up toward the crack and the cliff, scanned the coast in both directions. "Well, he's not here now. Which way did he go?"

Billy lifted his chin, two shiny wet rocks in his hands. "He was over there last time I saw him."

Nothing was there now but shimmering black lava for as far as I could see. "This is definitely not good."

Zach rubbed a hand over his mouth.

"He didn't go in the ocean, did he?" Casey said.

Sam and Billy shook their heads.

"Okay," I said. "Let's think about what we have. Last time anyone saw him, he was over there . . . so I say we start that way. You two stay right here. All right? Don't move."

The sun beat down on the shiny lava and bounced back up into my eyes as if it were coming off a window. There was no sand or scrub to soften the glare. I was stupid for not bringing a hat. My towel and T-shirt would have helped, but I'd dropped them.

"Tad!" Zach called. "Tad!"

To the right the ocean thumped against the rocky shore. I felt the first hint of panic.

We followed a faint trail heading into the endless desert of rock. Here the lava was curved and folded, dried and hardened smooth. There were fissures and holes and slits in the crust where animals could hide . . . if any animals ever came near this place.

"Tad!"

"We've come too far," Casey said. "There's nothing here but heat."

I glanced back toward camp. The ant-sized figures of Louie and Mike were heading down around the shoulder of the cliff. Sam and Billy were still in the tide pools.

My hands were sweating. I wiped them on my shorts.

"Tad!" Casey shouted again.

"He's not here. Let's go the other way."

Zach shaded his eyes and searched the landscape one last time, his face pinched.

Just as we turned to head back, we heard a voice.

"Help!"

It was muffled, somewhere behind us.

"Tad!" Zach yelled.

The rocky coast was deserted.

"Tad! Where are you?"

"Here!"

But there was nothing there.

"Where?"

"Here!"

We spread out and jumped over the rocks, searching. "Keep talking," I called. "Because we can't see you."

"I'm in a crack."

"There!" Casey said.

I squinted. "I don't see anything."

"I don't either," Zach said.

"See his shirt?"

"Whoa!" I said. A tiny shock of yellow was wedged into the black rock. "How'd he get in *there*?"

He was jammed into a crack so small and so tight it seemed impossible that he'd gotten into it at all. If he hadn't called, we'd never have found him. We hurried over, jumping cracks and sinkholes, careful not to step where the crust looked too thin and we could fall through.

We jumped down into the depression and squatted around the fissure. Tad was curled into a ball. All we could see was the back of his shirt. "Tad, come out," I said. "What are you doing in there?"

When I saw, I staggered back.

Zach and Casey scrambled away, too, dodging and ducking the wasps that swirled through the air and attacked the crack where Tad was wedged.

"Make them go away!" Tad yelped.

Zach dropped down as a wasp whizzed past his face.

"Tad," Casey said, "you got any food in there with you?"

"A can of peaches."

"An open can?"

"I was eating them when they attacked me."

Casey looked at me. "They want the sugar. Out here food is so scarce they could prob'ly smell those peaches from ten miles away." Casey hunched down. "Tad, you got to get rid of them."

"But I already ate the whole can."

"You still got the can in there?"

"Yeah."

"Throw it out, then."

"I can't. I'm stuck. I can't move my arms."

Casey tried to move closer, but the wasps got angrier. I pulled him back. "Don't get them mad at us, too."

Casey squatted and thought a moment. "Tad . . . listen, just shove it between your legs, if you can. Wiggle it till it falls out. We'll take it from there, okay?"

A moment later the tin can came tumbling out. The wasps swarmed onto it, fighting to get at the sticky juice drying inside.

Casey stood and searched the rocks. "Dylan, Zach, look for a stick."

A stick? Out here?

But Zach got lucky. He found a piece of driftwood and tossed it to Casey.

Casey inched toward the wasp-covered can and carefully worked the stick into the open end. Wasps buzzed off but came back, some landing on the stick, their stingers sagging with poison. Slowly, Casey lifted the peach can and carried it several yards inland, then set it down lightly. He left the stick in it and backed away.

The wasps stayed with the can.

"Okay, Tad, come out now. Hurry . . . we got to get out of here before they finish off the sugar. Next thing they'll want is the water in our eyes."

We helped him wiggle out. Two ugly wasp stings boiled on his neck and face. His arms were scratched from the lava fissure.

"Well, well," someone said.

I jumped, startled.

Louie and Mike stood on the rim of lava above us, Louie leaning forward with his hands on his knees. "Looks like the senior patrol loser found the lost boy."

9
WELTS
OF GUILT

Tad's eyes were swollen with tears. The stings must have really hurt. If what Casey said about the wasps going after the water in our eyes was true, then we had to start moving, fast.

Louie squatted above us on the rim. He looked at me and shook his head. "What a laugh you are. You can't even make two stupits stay together."

"Not your business, Louie," Casey said.

Louie turned to Casey and nailed him with his copper eyes. The skull and shark's tooth swung out over his chest. "That right?"

"We found him. Everything's fine."

Louie turned back to me. I felt like I was ten and had just

done something to screw up again. I couldn't look at him. He was right. I was a laugh. I'd let Zach mess up when I should have insisted he go back to Tad right away.

Louie stood and jumped into the depression.

Mike followed, easing down more slowly. I wondered if it bothered him to be Louie's pet dog. It sure bothered me.

"What's wrong with his face?" Mike said.

"Wasps," Casey said. "He got stung."

"I don't see any wasps."

Behind him they were starting to rise off the can. We had to move . . . *now.*

"So Mike," Louie said, not seeing the wasps either. "You should take over for this punk, ah?"

I edged back, ready to run for it if those wasps came for my eyes. Mike rubbed his chin. The wasps hovered, finished with the peach can. I took another step back.

Mike said, "Listen, don't say anything to Mr. Bellows or my dad. We could all get in trouble."

The wasps circled higher, leaving the peach can, moving on. I started to scramble up out of the depression.

Louie stopped me, his hand on my chest. "Who said you could go?"

I slapped his hand away. The wasps were coming.

He shoved me and I stumbled into Casey.

"Hey!" Casey said.

"You like some of that, too?"

The wasps circled higher and higher, spreading out, ready to attack. "Get out of my way," I said, pushing past Louie, stumbling out of the depression.

Louie came after me, his fists balled.

"Let him alone, Louie," Mike said. "No need get us in trouble, too, ah?"

"In my school you wouldn't last one day, haole," Louie called after me. "My friends would pick their teeth with your *bones*!"

The wasps zoomed down.

Casey, Zach, and Tad scrambled out after me. We ran, leaving Louie and Mike swatting, dodging, ducking, and yelping, and inside I laughed like crazy.

That night we sat around the campfire with light from the flames jumping on our faces. I glanced over at Tad's swollen stings. He was taking it like a man. So was Louie, who had three nasty welts on his arms and one on the back of his neck. Mike had miraculously escaped.

Earlier, when Reverend Paia and Mr. Bellows had returned from their hike down the coast, Mr. Bellows asked about the stings. "Got into some wasps" was all Louie said.

Mr. Bellows nodded. "My fault, Louie. I forgot to tell you about them . . . sorry."

Louie shrugged and looked at Tad. "We can take it, ah, brah?" He put a hand on Tad's head and ruffled his hair.

Tad nodded, grinning shyly.

Reverend Paia ducked into his tent and came back with a blue jar of Noxema. "I brought this for sunburn, but maybe it will help take some of the sting out."

Louie took the jar and opened it. "Smells good," he said,

digging a finger into the white paste. He plastered it on Tad's stings first, and then his own.

"Anything else I should know about, boys?" Mr. Bellows said.

I kept quiet. They got stung. Why say more? What happened today wasn't going to happen again, not on my watch.

"Dylan?"

I shook my head.

"Mike? Louie?"

I looked up. "Nothing else," Louie said.

"Great." Mr. Bellows rubbed his hands together. "Let's get dinner going."

We all avoided his eyes as he and Reverend Paia gathered up the driftwood they'd found on their hike and headed over to the fire pit.

"Thanks," I mumbled to Louie. "You didn't have to—"

He turned his face away and held up his hand. Without looking at me or anyone else, he strode over to his tent.

"What's with him?" Casey said.

"He doesn't like messing up in front of your dad," Mike said. "Believe it or not, he likes it here."

I snorted. "Right."

"Like I said, believe it or not."

"You like the way he uses you, Mike? Like his pet?"

Mike glared at me a moment, his eyes steady. "Nice," he said, and headed toward the camp in the coconut grove. The others followed him, heads down, silent.

I stayed where I was, my hands on my hips. Jeese, I thought. What a stupid thing for me to say.

Casey turned back to see if I was coming.

I shook my head and faced the ocean. A billow of clouds sat yellowing in a sun that would set on the other side of the island. I didn't know what to think. For sure I needed to apologize to Mike. He didn't deserve that.

When I looked back, I saw Louie alone, walking with his head down toward the grove. *He doesn't like messing up.* I grabbed a handful of pebbles and started thwacking them into the ocean. I didn't like messing up, either.

10
SPIRITS

That night we sat around a campfire built with driftwood. The flames burned a bright yellow-orange from the salt in the wood. The air was still warm, but it had cooled down, and the heat from the fire felt good. I sat on a rock with my arms folded into my stomach, leaning toward the jumping flames.

But my eyes were on Louie.

He stood across the fire, just beyond Billy, Tad, and Sam, who were looking over their shoulders at him. He knew they were looking.

Over and over, Louie threw his knife into a coconut tree. It landed each time with a point-perfect *thunk*. After each toss he slowly walked over to pull it out, glancing at me briefly, cleaning the pulp off the blade before going back to toss it again.

Thunk!

I got the feeling Mr. Bellows wanted to say something. But he was silent.

Thunk!

I looked away when Zach said, "Reverend, tell us a story." Billy, Sam, and Tad turned back to the fire.

Reverend Paia stretched and yawned. He'd been keeping an eye on Louie, too. But Mr. Bellows was the leader, and if anyone was going to say anything, it had to be him.

"What do you have in mind, Zach?" Reverend Paia said.

"Something spooky?"

"Yeah, yeah," Billy said. "Spooky."

Thunk!

"Well . . . let me think."

Because he was a minister, Reverend Paia was full of stories, and he could really tell the scary ones. Mike could, too, and he used to tell them all the time before Louie showed up. I guessed he thought it wasn't cool now.

Thunk!

"Tell them about the two brothers and the night marchers, Pop. They've been seen around here, right?" Mike glanced at Sam, Billy, and Tad, adding in a whisper, "They come out at night, you know. And if you look directly at them . . . you die."

Thunk!

"Yah!" Billy said, grinning.

Reverend Paia chuckled. "Don't scare them, Mike."

"No," Billy said. "Scare us!"

"Well," Reverend Paia said, leaning forward, pinching

his jaw with his fingers as if he were about to reveal a long-held secret.

Thunk!

"Louie," Mr. Bellows said, "why don't you come sit by the fire now? I think that tree has enough holes in it."

Louie pulled the blade out and wiped the tip on his shorts. He looked at me one last time, then shrugged and put the knife back into its leather sheath and stuck it in his back pocket.

"I think you'll like the Reverend's stories," Mr. Bellows added. "Come on, sit."

Louie found a spot on the sand behind Sam, Billy, and Tad. He sat with his knees up and his arms crossed over them, the blank why-am-I-here look plastered on his face.

Likes it here, huh, Mike?

"Well," Reverend Paia said, glancing around at us. "I've actually never seen any night marchers, you understand. Sightings are rare. But I've spoken to people who have . . . out of the corners of their eyes, of course, because Mike is right. If you look directly at them, they won't let you live to tell about it. That's the first thing you need to know about night marchers—if you see them, don't look directly at them. Never, never, never."

Reverend Paia let a moment of silence swell.

"You sure you want to hear this? Might give you night-mares."

"We can take it, Reverend," Zach said.

Tad got up. "Wait. Be right back." He hurried over to his tent.

Louie lay back on the sand and clasped his hands behind his head, gazing up at the stars. He rolled to the side, pulled the knife out of his pocket, and set it on his chest.

I poked the fire with a stick. Sparks flew, fading into the night. How did this day get so messed up?

Tad returned with his backpack. He set it down on the sand and used it as a backrest. Hoping no one would notice, he slowly pulled out his blue blanket.

"Okay," Reverend Paia said, holding up one finger. "First, this area was once a sacred place. Maybe it still is. There's an old Hawaiian *heiau* just down the coast. You boys know what that is? A place where the old Hawaiians held their sacred ceremonies. Spirits wander all over this area."

"Even now?" Tad said.

"Even now. They never really leave, you see. This is their home."

"Are they the night marchers?" Billy asked.

Reverend Paia opened his hands. "I don't know . . . but listen, I heard of two brothers who came down here to Halape one time a while back. They came to fish, planned to stay three nights. But they only stayed one. Actually, only one brother did. The other one . . . well . . ."

"The other one vanished . . . never seen again," Mike said, almost in a whisper.

Reverend Paia shook his head sadly. "They'd just gotten into their sleeping bags on that first night. It was late, about midnight. They'd fished into the darkness and were tired. Their fire was just a dim glow when the younger brother popped up on his elbow and nodded toward the slope—the same one we came down today. 'Look!' was all he said."

Billy and Tad turned and looked up at Pu'u Kapukapu, now a massive black silhouette against the starry sky.

Reverend Paia went on. "The older boy sat up to see what his brother was pointing at. In the distance he saw a snake of flashlights winding down the trail from the pali above. He watched the lights, at first thinking it was more fishermen, or maybe some campers coming in late. But then he realized they weren't lights at all . . . they were torches. *'Get down!'* he gasped, pushing his brother into the sand. 'Those are night marchers!' And the younger brother says, 'Get outta here, there's no such thing.'

"But he got down low anyway, because he wasn't sure about that, and his brother really did seem scared.

" 'If they come close,' the older one said, 'you got to lie flat with your face in the sand, and whatever you do, don't look at them, promise me. . . . *Do not look at them.* . . . If we're lucky, they won't see us.'

"So . . . they wait . . . and wait . . . crouching down behind the rocks with their faces in the sand."

Reverend Paia pointed to a spot just past Louie. "Maybe they were right over there behind those rocks."

Tad rocked back and forth, hugging his blue blanket. Billy had his T-shirt up over his head, laughing.

Louie snickered, his eyes covered in the crook of his arm.

"What's so funny?" Casey said.

Louie lifted his arm and peeked up. "I just thinking about tonight when I going hear you crying from your tents— 'Mommy!' "

"Shuddup!" Zach said.

Mr. Bellows smiled and tossed another piece of driftwood

onto the fire. Louie put his arm back over his eyes, chuckling.

"So what happened, Reverend?" Zach said.

Reverend Paia waited a moment to get everyone's complete attention. Silence had a way of doing that. "So, as the line of torches came closer, the older brother dug deeper into the sand and covered his head with his arms. But the younger one just had to see if they were real. Maybe night marchers weren't ghosts at all, but real people trying to scare other people away. So he peeked up to look and . . . *boom!*"

Everyone jumped. Billy yelped.

"Right there in front of him were the night marchers, their torches shining on his face! The guy's mouth was hanging open, because they had sunken holes where their eyes should have been. And they were floating because they had no feet. The guy tried to scream, but all that would come out was this choking sound, like he couldn't breathe!"

Reverend Paia put his hands around his neck and made gagging sounds. "Aggh, aggh!"

Sam's eyes bugged out. "Ho!"

Reverend Paia jumped back into he story. "The older brother with his face in the dirt was shaking, because he could hear his brother choking, but he knew that if he looked up, he would die. He hoped his brother's noises were only the sounds of fear and nothing was happening to him.

"Suddenly, everything . . . went . . . silent."

Louie raised his arm off his eyes and peeked up again.

"The older brother waited for fifteen minutes," Reverend Paia whispered. "He was afraid to move, even an inch. Then . . . slowly, slowly, slowly . . . he looked up."

Reverend Paia shook his head, as if recalling a painful memory.

"What!" Billy said.

"Gone . . . his brother was gone. And so were the night marchers and their torches. All over Halape there was only the land, the ocean, and the stars, as peaceful as it is right now."

We all gazed up.

"He never saw his younger brother again. He no longer existed."

"Wow," Billy whispered.

"That older brother is an old man now. But he never went fishing again. Anywhere."

"Ho, man," Sam said.

Tad was hidden under his blue blanket.

"Is that true, Reverend?" Billy said. "I mean, really?"

Reverend Paia stared into the fire, flame light wobbling on his face. He shook his head once, thinking deeply. "Who's to say, Billy? That's what I heard."

I wondered if he believed . . . Naah. Not a reverend.

Louie looked as if he'd fallen asleep, the knife resting on his chest.

"So if you see torches tonight," Mike added, "stay inside your tents. You come out . . . nobody ever going see you again."

Louie snorted.

I stood and brushed the sand from the back of my shorts. "Good story, Reverend."

"Yeah," the others said, all getting up to head to their tents. "Good story."

Louie eased up on one elbow. "Watch out tonight when you go out for make *shi-shi,* ah?"

Mike laughed.

"Come on, Louie," Billy pleaded.

Louie tapped Billy's leg with his foot. "No worry, brah. I protec' you." He pushed himself up and headed over to his tent with Mike.

Mr. Bellows kicked sand over the last of the fire.

Casey, Zach, and I said goodnight and walked over to our shelter. "Man, that was creepy," Zach said.

Casey flicked on his flashlight. "He just made it up."

"How do you know?"

"Well . . . think about it. How could the older brother know that the night marchers had sunken eyes and no feet if the only one who actually saw them disappeared? The older brother never looked up, right? That's why he lived. He couldn't know."

"Hey, you're right."

"Of course I am, and anyway, there's no such thing as night marchers."

I wasn't so sure. Who knew what went on around us that we couldn't see? This place could be crawling with spirits. I looked up at Pu'u Kapukapu and shivered. "Let's talk about something else, all right? I don't want to go to sleep with creepy things on my mind."

"Me either," Casey said.

"I thought you said there were no such things as night marchers," Zach said.

Casey grinned, shining the flashlight up under his chin. "You never know."

Late that night I bolted up.

Something was crawling on my face.

I scrambled out of my sleeping bag and grabbed my glasses and flashlight.

Roaches!

All over the dirt floor of the shelter, scattering in the light.

Casey propped himself up on one elbow, blinking into the light.

"Look!" I said.

Roaches the size of my big toe were running for cover, ugly brown, with slick, shiny wings. Casey flew out of his sleeping bag and stood in his boxers. "I hate those things!"

We slapped the roaches out with anything we could grab, sprayed new moats of bug repellent around us, and tried to go back to sleep.

This *place*. Jeese.

Later still, I woke again.

I didn't know why; just a feeling.

I sat up, my sleeping bag twisted around me. Casey was a dark lump snoring on the other side of the shelter. Nothing moved outside by Zach's tent.

So, so quiet.

There was only the sea, breathing in, breathing out. Hushed rolling waves out in the blackness.

But something had awakened me.

I got up and slipped out into the night.

Pu'u Kapukapu loomed above, solid black. Brilliant stars winked in the moonless sky beyond it. The soft ocean. The shadow of the coconut grove. Zach's tent. All was as it should have been. I was about to go back into the shelter when I saw the silhouettes on the crest of the cliff.

Two dogs.

11
THE HEAT EQUATION

Early the next morning Mr. Bellows and Reverend Paia took Sam, Billy, Tad, and Zach on a hike up the coast, where they would stop to see the old Hawaiian heiau Reverend Paia had mentioned. Casey said there had been human sacrifices there in the olden days, but I didn't believe it. After that, they'd hike on to identify plants and sea life and work on some of their advancement requirements.

Mr. Bellows wanted to get started early so they could work before the sun became more of an enemy than a friend. After ten, they would fry. Where they were going, shade didn't exist.

"Mr. Bellows," I said, "while you're gone, can me and Casey swim out to the island?"

Mr. Bellows thought as he boiled catchment water for his

canteen over the small propane stove. "I'd really rather you waited until we get back."

I glanced out toward the island, called Keaoi, which was little more than a mound of rocks rising out of the sea. An easy swim, about fifty yards.

"We'll be careful, Dad," Casey said.

Mr. Bellows turned off the propane and looked up. "All right, fine . . . but listen, you can only do it if Mike and Louie go with you. In fact . . ." He looked back over his shoulder. "Mike, Louie, come here a minute."

"Sir?" Mike said.

"Dylan and Casey want to swim out to the island today. I said they could, but only if you and Louie went with them. That okay with you?"

"No problem, Mr. Bellows."

"Good. Since you four will be here alone while we're gone, I'd like you to stick together. That'd make me feel better."

"Sure, we can do that."

There goes the day, I thought. But I really wanted to swim to the island, even if Louie had to be there.

Mr. Bellows poured boiled water into his canteen, then into Reverend Paia's. The younger Scouts were doing the same at their own fire. I still had a little fresh water left, and was drinking it as slowly as possible. Not a great idea, considering how badly you needed to stay hydrated down here. But just the smell of catchment water made me gag.

Mr. Bellows stuck his canteen into his small day pack, then slapped on his Dodgers cap. "You remember the heat equation, Casey?"

70

"High temperature plus high humidity plus physical work equals heat illness or death."

"Exactly. Remember that, and stay hydrated."

"Can we use the propane to boil catchment water?"

"Sure, just be sure you turn it off afterwards."

I looked up, feeling someone's eyes on me. Louie smiled. Did he know I was trying to make my fresh water last? I frowned and looked away.

Louie smirked.

By seven-thirty the younger guys were ready for their hike. I wondered, if Louie was going to be a Scout, why wasn't Mr. Bellows taking him, too? Mr. Bellows hadn't let the rest of us slide like that.

"Men," Mr. Bellows said, giving us a snappy marine salute. Except for when we had a formal meeting, he preferred that salute to the three-fingered Scout one.

We gave him full-on *semper fidelis* salutes back. Except for Louie, who stood leaning against a coconut tree with his arms crossed.

They left, a slow line snaking out over the rocks.

"Time to swim!" I said.

Casey and I went back to the shelter.

I took another sip of fresh water. I could have guzzled two gallons. Already it was hot and my throat was dry. Was the heat equation starting to work on me? Maybe death was just around the corner. I drained my canteen. Now I *had* to drink catchment water. But not just yet.

We yanked on our swim shorts and ran down to the small beach. The ocean was calling me. . . . Dylan, come swim.

Louie and Mike were still at the main campsite. Mike was

putting snacks the young guys had left out into plastic bags so the bugs wouldn't get to them. Louie was throwing his knife into another tree. Mike got him to stop and the two of them picked trash up around the coconut grove, taking their time.

"Mike!" I shouted. "Let's go!"

"Stop yelling," Casey said. "It'll only make them take longer."

We sat looking at the sea glittering like a field of jewels in the sun. "So," I said, glancing back at the grove. Mike and Louie weren't in a hurry to go swimming. "You were telling me about how your dad found Louie in a warehouse."

"I don't know if I should be telling anybody about that."

"Too late. You already did. Come on, Case, why did he run away from home?"

Casey grumbled, then said, "In a way, he didn't."

"What does that mean?"

"His parents didn't even know he was gone."

I gaped. "Get out of here."

"True. . . . See . . . according to Dad, Louie's family is kind of . . . well . . . as Dad said it, the family had completely disintegrated."

"Meaning?"

"The mother and father were like zombies. Dad said they were so depressed they had no idea Louie had left the house to live somewhere else. Anyway, his older brother did it all the time."

"Why were they depressed?"

Casey shrugged. "Out of work. Drinking. Drugs. No money, no hope . . . who knows?"

I whistled, low. "What about his brother?"

Casey glanced back to make sure Louie and Mike weren't coming up on us. "Kind of a nasty guy. One day he got in a fight with the dad, beat him up, and took all his money. Put the dad in the hospital. The cops arrested Louie's brother, and he ended up in youth correction for a while."

"Hoo," I said, shaking my head.

"No kidding."

"What about the dad? He all right?"

"I guess, but after that, he started sliding. Him and the mother both, straight downhill. Eventually they got so out of it that Louie couldn't take it anymore, so he left and found that warehouse and moved in."

"And he still went to school?"

"Yeah, and he got that job at Jimmy's Place. He gave almost all his cash to his parents to pay the bills, because neither of them had a job."

Ho, I thought, the schoolkid taking care of the parents. Paying the bills.

"When payday came, he cashed his check, bought some food for his hideaway, then took the rest and left it on the kitchen table at home. His parents just picked it up and spent it . . . didn't even wonder where it came from."

"Can you really be that far out of it?"

"Looks like it. Dad's seen other people like that."

I lifted my head as a breeze blew in off the water. It felt like a silk scarf flowing over my face. "So what did your dad do? I mean, about Louie?"

"Made a deal with him. If Louie went back home, Dad wouldn't turn him in for trespassing."

"And Louie just did it?"

Casey nodded. "Not only that, he was respectful about it, and that's why Dad took a liking to him. He doesn't see that very often. Dad went out of his way to get someone from social services to work with Louie's parents, and he goes by once or twice a week, too. Takes them fresh fish when he can get it, fruit, stuff like that. But here's the kicker . . . part of the deal was that Louie had to come to Scouts."

"Jeese," I spat. *"Why?"*

Casey lifted his shoulders. "I guess he thinks Scouts will help him."

"Or ruin us."

"Maybe."

"No relatives?"

"Guess not."

I shook my head. "Why Louie? Your dad must run into a hundred tough guys every week. Got to be more to it."

Casey tossed a pebble into the ocean. "Most of those other guys go in and out of the police station five times a day. Dad said Louie was clean as a bar of soap."

"Clean?"

"No police record. . . . Did you know he walks to the meetings?"

I squinted at Casey.

"You didn't know?"

"Never thought about it. He just shows up . . . when he comes."

"You saw how far away his house is."

I nodded.

"Five miles," Casey said. "That's how far he walks for Scouts."

"Not for Scouts, Case . . . for your dad. Louie couldn't care less about Scouts."

"That's probably true." Casey cocked his head and thought a moment. "You know, Dad could be the first guy in Louie's life that ever gave a rip about him."

"But what—"

"Shhh. Here they come."

I looked over my shoulder. Louie and Mike were slouching toward us, shirtless. A pudge and a muscleman. The shark's tooth hanging around Louie's neck made me think of the shark Mr. Bellows had warned us about. The skull just gave me the creeps.

"You ready?" Mike said.

Casey stood and took off his T-shirt. "Ready yesterday."

I couldn't help looking at Louie. It was as if there was some kind of weird magnet between us. As hard as I tried, it just wasn't possible to ignore him, or even pretend I could.

"Whatchoo looking at, haole?" he said. The muscles in his jaw rippled. His eyes were empty of anything good.

I turned away, shaking my head.

"You like go round with me, punk?" he said.

"No."

"Good choice."

12
SHARK

The water was warm, calm, and so clear you could see the bottom as easily as looking through glass. Which was good, because there were a zillion *wana* down there, spiky black sea urchins that would stab poison into your foot if you stepped on them.

Inside I felt like a smoldering dump fire. Who needs sour looks and someone trying to push you around, ruining your life? I'd come here to get away from that.

"Out of my way," Louie said, shoving past us.

He went in first and bobbed out awkwardly, then started churning up a lot of foam as he dog-paddled toward the island. Well, I'll be, I thought. Mr. Bad Man can't swim. That made me feel better.

Louie splashed across the water to where he could touch bottom, and made it up onto the island without stepping on any wana.

The rest of us glided around underwater like fish, me with my glasses clutched in my hand, the fishing-line cord curled around my wrist. I did my best to make the swim look effortless, as if I'd been born to the sea.

The island was just a pile of rocks with a little dirt and a handful of weeds. We climbed onto it and sat in the sun. I blew the water off my glasses and put them back on.

Wow . . . what a view!

Across the way, our camp in the coconut grove looked tiny under the massive cliff. The wall was a thousand feet high, a face of boulders that dwarfed everything below it. I scanned the ridgeline, remembering the night before. "Last night I saw two dogs up there. They were looking down on us."

Casey shaded his eyes and gazed up at Pu'u Kapukapu. "Maybe they were those same ones we saw before."

"That was my thought, too."

After a pause, Louie said, "They following us."

I glanced at him.

He turned away, looked at the ocean.

Mike said, "Prob'ly hoping to snack on our food."

Minutes passed in silence. I studied the desolate landscape, the southernmost point of the entire United States. It was beautiful . . . in a barren kind of way.

"Ho!" Mike said. "Look."

Just offshore, weaving its way in and out of the shallow

waters between where we sat and our camp, was a sleek gray fin.

Shark.

I felt my hair rise, watching it move. There was a round hole in its fin, a wound that had puckered and healed discolored. The shark was nosing through the reef, feeding, minding its own business.

But sharks are sharks. One scent of blood, sweat, or fear and they could go nuts. This one wasn't that big, but it was big enough to make my gut twist into a knot.

"That's going to make swimming back interesting," Casey said.

"Wait it out," Mike said. "It'll go away."

I put up my hand. "Don't move. If it knows we're here, it might wait around for us to get in the water."

Louie laughed. "Right."

"Well, maybe it will. What do you know?"

"Sharks don't think."

"It smells us," Mike said. "Lunch."

"Shuddup, Mike," Casey said.

Louie stood, looking at the shark, steady and cool. "You ready fo' swim back?"

Casey's jaw dropped. "You *crazy*?"

"You scared of it?"

The shark was gliding right in front of us now. The hole in its fin looked like a battle scar.

Casey shaded his eyes and looked up at Louie. "Not scared, Louie . . . smart."

I nodded, not looking at Louie.

Mike, too, seemed to agree. He stood when Louie did, but made no move to go near the water. "You joking, right?"

"I don't believe this," Louie said. "*All* of you are scared? The shark not even big as you, Mike . . . look."

The turning fin swirled the surface like a spoon stirring water, snaking around. "Small sharks still have sharp teeth," I said. "Maybe you don't mind losing your foot, but I sure do."

Louie looked long at me, then said, "Stupid four-eye no-guts haole."

"Shuddup, Louie," Casey said. "I don't like that shark, either."

"*Two* no-guts haoles."

Casey shook his head.

Mike kept his mouth shut, but I could tell he was worried. Louie wasn't stupid, but I didn't doubt he'd go out and swim with that shark just to prove he was a big man and we weren't.

"We go, Mike," Louie said. "Your senior patrol loser said we buddies, right? We got to stick together."

"Yeah, but . . . *tst* . . . how's about this time instead of me sticking with you, you stick with *me*?"

Louie glared at him.

Mike sighed and started toward the water.

Louie waggled his eyebrows at me and Casey. "Watch how men do it."

Louie waded in up to his waist, bending over to study the wana, stepping around them. The shark sensed him there and scooted off, then turned and circled back. Louie watched it as he slipped into the water, to his waist, his chest, his neck. He started paddling, slapping his way across to the beach. I cringed. Splashing like that was one of the worst things you could do—the shark would think you were a fish in trouble and attack.

Mike watched, open-mouthed, knee-deep.

The shark meandered toward Louie. Curious.

Louie turned and hit the water hard with his open hand. The shark darted away.

Then came back.

But by then Louie had made it to the beach. He slogged out and shouted back, "No sweat, brah."

"Right," Mike mumbled. "No sweat."

"You don't have to do it," I said.

"Shuddup."

Mike waited until the shark was as far away as it was going to get, then dove in and swam as if ten barracudas were nipping at his toes. Only then did I realize how strong a hold Louie had on Mike.

The shark nosed closer, more or less chasing him.

"Man, that's stupid!" Casey said.

"That shark is *really* curious now."

"All right!" Louie said, slapping hands with Mike as Mike scrambled up the beach.

"Easy!" Mike shouted to me and Casey, now thrilled to find himself alive. He and Louie whooped it up on the sand, rubbing their bravery in our faces.

"Look at those morons," I said.

We sat.

The shark swam, in, out, in, out.

"Let's go together," Casey said. "Make it look like we might be too much to mess with."

"I don't like the word *might*."

"Yeah."

"Or we could just wait until it goes away."

"That would be the smart thing."

Minutes passed. The sun blasted down, and the water on my back evaporated to crystals of salt. The shark seemed to have all the time in the world, cruising, waiting.

"But we're not very smart, are we," I said.

"No."

We got up.

The shark seemed to know what we were thinking, never straying from the path between us and the beach. Small whirlpools erupted around its fin whenever it turned. I could even see its eye, looking. I wiped my palms on my damp shorts.

Casey tossed a rock at it. The shark jolted. Casey threw another one and it shot out to sea.

Gone.

Tired of this game.

We jumped in and swam like spooked sardines. Near shore, something rough in the water rubbed up against me, like sandpaper. . . . Shark skin!

I yelped, beating at it with my fists.

Casey hit the sand and stumbled up the beach, looking back, shouting, "Run, Dylan! Run!"

The thing grabbed my legs. "Get it off! Get it off!"

It fell away as I staggered ashore, my heart slamming in my chest. I looked back.

At an old submerged palm frond.

Louie and Mike laughed so hard they fell on the sand and cried.

13
SHADOWS

I grabbed my T-shirt and left. Casey ran to catch up. Louie and Mike whooped behind us, having as much fun as rats in a trash pile.

"Dylan, wait up!"

The sun was merciless. In minutes the water on my back was nothing but salt crystals. I yanked my T-shirt on.

"Forget those idiots," Casey said. "Let's go swim in the crack."

"Anywhere but here."

We hiked up and stood on the rim, looking down the trail at the still, green water. I hesitated, thinking about Mr. Bellows. How mad would he get if he caught us split up like this?

I glanced back to see where Louie and Mike were.

Nowhere. Maybe in their tent.

"Who cares," I mumbled.

"What?"

"We were supposed to stay together, remember?"

Casey looked back and shrugged.

"Forget it," I said. If Casey wasn't worried, why should I be? We headed into the crack.

The water sparkled in the sun. Algae grew like fuzz on submerged rocks, yellow in the sunlight. Deeper into the shadiest parts of the crack, the water was black and still.

I stepped in, ankle-deep. It was so cool and soothing that all thoughts of Louie, Mike, and the soggy palm frond vanished. "You got to go a long way to find something to beat this, Case."

He stepped in. "That's for dang sure. Those little punks are going to come straight up here after that hike . . . if they got any feet left, anyway. Dad's kind of a slave driver."

"He doesn't feel pain."

"That's good, I guess . . . for a detective."

"Fighting bad guys all day long, you need that."

"He doesn't fight. He uses his brain. The fighting is for the big guys, like Billy's dad."

"He's a cop?"

"No, but he's big."

A rock zooped down into the water. We looked up. How'd they get here so fast?

"Whatchoo ladies doing down there?" Louie called. Mike stood next to him.

"Stop with the rocks," I said. "Somebody could get hurt!"

Louie picked up another one and lobbed it into the water just close enough to make me nervous.

I ripped off my T-shirt, tossed it on the dry rocks, and set my glasses on top of it. "Case—swim back into the dark part where they can't see us."

Casey dropped his shirt near mine, and we swam deep into the crack. Looking back was like looking out of a cave. The water was half in shadow, half in the sun. Our shirts were bright spots on the rocks across the way. The trail beyond led up to a patch of blue sky. Without my glasses everything was fuzzy, but I could see shapes and colors and make things out well enough to identify them.

"Maybe they'll go away," Casey said.

"In your dreams."

Mike and Louie appeared in the patch of sky at the top of the trail. They slouched down, joking and shoving and making a lot of noise.

"Our shadows," Casey said.

"Our nightmares."

Louie squatted at the edge of the water. He picked up my glasses and dangled them on the cord, then put them on. "Mike, Mike, where you stay?" He stuck out his hands as if he were blind.

"Over here."

"Which one? I see four Mikes."

"That's because you got four eyes now."

Louie snickered. "You funny, brah." He took the glasses off and blinked. "I can see! I can see!"

"Put those back!" I shouted. "Unless you want to carry me home, because I can't hike out of here without them."

"Hoo, sissy-boy. I going join Girl Scouts before I carry you."

"They wouldn't let you in," I said, and Casey laughed.

Louie tossed my glasses back onto my T-shirt. He picked up another rock and bounced it in his hand. Just before he threw it, Mike grabbed his arm and pointed his chin back up the trail.

A man was staring down at us from the mouth of the crack.

A man in a cowboy hat. On a horse. Four other horsemen and a packhorse rose into view behind him.

14
MASA

"Paniolos?" Casey whispered.

I gaped up the trail. "There aren't any cows down here."

The lead man dismounted and let the reins fall at his feet. His horse nudged the ground, ripping up a chunk of dry weeds. The other riders stayed in the saddle.

For a moment, none of us moved.

Finally, Louie dropped the rock and headed up the trail with Mike.

Casey and I swam back to the rocks. I picked up my glasses and T-shirt and put them on. We started up. Now the riders were in focus. The lead man looked about fifty. He wore jeans, a black T-shirt, and scarred brown cowboy boots. He pushed the brim of his sweat-stained straw hat back on his head with his thumb. The hat had a red-feathered band around it.

The paniolo's skin was leather brown, and worn from a lifetime outdoors. A sparse patch of hair hung from his chin.

We nodded at each other.

"Name's Masa," he said, a smile in his eyes. I liked him instantly.

"Dylan," I said, nodding. "And this is Casey."

He dipped his head to Casey. "We came to fish. How's about you folks?"

"Scout camp," Mike said, then lifted his chin toward the other cowboys. "How . . . how'd you get here?"

"Trucked up to the trailhead and rode down. We from a ranch in Kau."

I glanced back up at the cliff. "You came down that trail on *horseback*?"

"Just now. . . . You boys here by yourselfs?"

"No," Casey said. "There's more. We're camped in the grove. My dad's the scoutmaster. He went down the coast."

Masa turned toward the ocean. "You mind if we set up in that grove?"

Casey shrugged. "Fine with me. My dad will like the company."

Masa grinned. "You boys like to fish?"

"With a spinner," Mike said.

Louie nodded. "My uncle has a boat."

Masa turned to me and Casey. "How's about you two?"

"Never done much fishing," I said.

"What? Your daddy never take you?"

"He's not home much."

"My dad took me deep-sea fishing once," Casey said. "I never been so sick in my life."

Masa chuckled. "You get used to that. We going fish nighttime, with a light. Fish come right up, see what that light is all about. Like in the before time . . . *papio, taape, ulua*. The fish not scared of you here."

"Taape?" Mike said.

"Blueline snapper. Good fish."

Behind Masa the other cowboys leaned toward us, their forearms crossed over their pommels.

"Watch out by that island," I said. "There's a shark."

Masa raised an eyebrow. "Had a hole in the fin?"

"How'd you know?"

Masa grinned. "That's Fred."

"What?"

"He's been around Halape long time. Some say two hundred years."

Louie snorted.

Masa glanced at him. "Maybe more. Fred protects the bay, and you, too, if you get into trouble."

"Sharks don't protect people," Louie said. "They eat um." He grinned and looked at Mike.

Masa studied Louie. "You sure about that, boy?"

Louie didn't answer.

"How come it has a hole in its fin?" I said.

Masa looked at Louie a moment longer, then turned toward me. "Some fool shot it." Masa smiled. "That wasn't too smart."

"Why?"

He took off his hat and wiped the sweat from the inside

band with a finger. His short hair was black, peppered with gray, and his scalp was eerily white from wearing the hat all the time. He put the hat back on. "One time two guys came down here. Mainland guys. One of them had a pistol, for protection."

"From what?"

"Good question. Anyway, they wanted to go swimming, and like you, they saw Fred. Fred was just curious, you know? He likes company. So Fred came in close to check out his visitors. The one guy got his gun and shot him in the fin. You seen the hole. Fred took off and they went swimming. But he came back."

"And attacked them?"

"No, no . . . he came back later, at night while they sleeping . . . lying on the sand in their sleeping bags."

We waited for more. Masa took his time.

"Well, what happened?" Mike said.

Masa looked sideways, as if checking to make sure no one would hear. "About two o'clock in the morning," he whispered, "the guy with the gun wen' fly up! *Boom!*"

We all jumped.

Masa went on. "The guy scramble out of that bag and reach for his gun."

"Ho," Mike said. "What was it?"

"Something bumped him." Masa held up two fingers. "Two things happened. One, his gun was gone. Two, the guy's finger was frozen stiff. Trigger finger."

"Yai," Mike whispered.

"You just made that up, right?" I said.

"No, boy. True story. But here's the end of it—the guy's

finger stayed stiff all the way until the second they hiked across the national park line. Then—*pop!*—the finger wen' unstiff."

Louie burst into a laugh.

Mike and Casey grinned.

Masa raised his eyebrows. "Obviously, you boys never heard of the ghost shark of Halape."

"Pssh," Louie spat.

Masa seemed so sincere I didn't know what to think. The other cowboys looked amused.

"Of course, Fred is just the name we gave him," Masa went on. "He's got a Hawaiian name, but none of us were around two hundred years ago to find out what it was. But don't be fooled, Fred is for real. An old Hawaiian spirit lives inside that shark. You can swim right up to him and he won't bother you. He likes people, actually. It gets lonely around here. If he could, he would talk your ear off, I bet."

"Come on," Louie scoffed.

"I tell you what, boy. . . . What's your name?"

"Louie."

"Louie, listen . . . we going down by the trees, get set up. Then you come with us and we go swim. I show you Fred is Fred and not a shark like you think of a shark. How's about that?"

"Naah," Louie said. "No need."

Masa smiled and nodded. "Well, you change your mind, you come get me, ah?"

"Yeah, sure."

Masa clicked his tongue and his horse stepped closer to him. He picked up the reins and remounted. He tipped his hat and turned the horse toward the sea, the other paniolos following. And us, right behind them.

They unsaddled and brushed the horses down and carried the gear from the packhorse into the shade of the small cabin near the grove.

"You going to sleep in the cabin?" I asked.

"Black widows in there. We going sleep under the stars. When you boys came? Just today, or what?"

"Yesterday."

"Then you saw the stars. Hard to believe, ah?"

"Saw some dogs, too," I said.

"Dogs?"

"Wild ones . . . up there." I turned and pointed to the cliff. "I saw them at the trailhead, too . . . back when we started."

Masa's face turned serious. "What they looked like?"

"Well, one was big and black. The other was a small white one. Kind of skinny, too, and scraggy. I thought it was pretty strange to see dogs in this rocky place."

Masa glanced at the other paniolos. One was studying the ridgeline.

"What?" I said.

"We first spotted those dogs about two years ago," Masa said. "I think they been around here long time, too. Like Fred. But that small one . . ."

Masa hesitated. When he went on, his tone was quietly respectful. "What I think, is that white one is Pele."

I stepped back. Get serious! Pele was a ghost, a Hawaiian myth, a legend, not someone who was actually alive, and surely not a small white dog.

"Pele?" Casey echoed.

"Unreal," Louie said, throwing up his hands. "You no can see he's joking?" He elbowed Mike. "We go make a campfire. You cooking tonight, remember?"

"Yeah, but . . ."

Louie had to pull Mike away, Mike glancing back as they headed toward the fire pit.

"Of all you boys," Masa said, "that one should believe. Look like he got Hawaiian blood."

I studied the ridge. "Something woke me last night. I just had this . . . this *feeling*. Everything was quiet, everyone was sleeping. Still, I had that feeling, so I went out to look around . . . and there they were, looking down on us. Same dogs we saw up on top, I'm sure of it."

"It was a warning," Masa whispered.

"A *warning*?"

Masa nodded, looking grim. A two-hundred-year-old shark didn't spook him one little bit. But that small white dog sure did.

For the rest of the day I couldn't stop thinking about that, even after Mr. Bellows returned from the hike. Who was this guy Masa? Was he fooling with us, like Louie said? Or trying to scare us away so they could have Halape to themselves? No, that didn't feel right.

Now I was starting to get spooked.

I closed my eyes and pinched the bridge of my nose. Bad thoughts can take you down a deep, dark hole if you're not careful.

15
PELE

That night around the campfire we roasted marshmallows on sticks. Billy tended a nasty blister on his heel, and Mr. Bellows had a cut on his shin where he'd slipped and hit a jagged rock. Sam, Tad, Zach, and Reverend Paia were so beat I thought they might fall asleep sitting up.

"That hike too much for you, Pop?" Mike said.

Reverend Paia grunted, too tired to respond.

In the twilight across the grove, the paniolos had their own campfire going. Soon the last glow of sundown faded away and turned the ocean black.

We sat quietly around the campfire. Everyone was worn out. And full. Mike had actually planned a decent meal of potatoes, carrots, onions, a magic potion of spices, and hamburger kept on ice that was nearly melted. We each sliced and combined all this, wrapped portions in aluminum foil, and stuck them in the fire to cook. I could have eaten five of them.

Mr. Bellows went over to invite the paniolos to join us around the fire, but only Masa and a round-faced smiley guy named Cappy came back with him. The other cowboys had already gone fishing down the coast, their lamps glowing in the distance.

"This is Reverend Paia, father of Mike over there," Mr. Bellows said, and Masa reached out to shake.

"Nice to meet you, Reverend."

"Same here," Reverend Paia said. "Have a seat."

Masa and Cappy eased down around the fire. "You and John are the first Boy Scout leaders I've ever met," Masa said. The sound of Mr. Bellows's first name gave me a small jolt. I hardly ever heard him called anything but Mr. Bellows or Dad.

"First time for everything."

Masa smiled.

Mr. Bellows swept his hand toward the rest of us. "Meet Troop Seventy-seven, small, but mighty. We're out of Hilo."

"Did they clean this place up?" Masa said. "I never seen Halape so spotless."

"I think that was the big boys," Mr. Bellows said.

Masa nodded toward Louie and Mike. "Nice job."

"Were you ever a Boy Scout, Masa?" Mr. Bellows asked.

Masa shook his head gravely. "No, I grew up on a ranch in Kau. Same place I work now. Too far for anything like that. I was chasing cows and pigs by the time I was ten. Cappy, too. Me and him go back to the beginning of time, ah, Cappy?"

"Long time."

Reverend Paia poked the glowing coals with a stick. "It's so easy for some boys to get sucked into a bad way of life, you know? Which is why I'm glad these boys want to be Scouts. . . . We have a good time."

Mr. Bellows nodded, firelight wobbling on his face. He knew way too much about how bad it could get. He saw it all day long in his work.

"Mr. Masa," Casey said. "Tell us more about the small white dog."

Mr. Bellows looked up. "What dog is that?"

"Dylan saw it."

Masa shook his head.

The younger guys perked up, sensing something interesting. Louie stretched out on the sand, his head propped up on a coconut wrapped in his sweatshirt.

"Pele," Masa said softly, looking out into the darkness.

Mr. Bellows raised his eyebrows.

"One of your boys saw a small white dog last night," Masa said, seeing his confusion. "Down on this end of the island, that means something. You see, Pele often appears as a small white dog."

Mr. Bellows shifted to face Masa. "Listen up, boys," he said. "What can you tell us about Pele, Masa?"

"Where did you grow up, John?"

"Arizona. My wife and I came here after I got out of the marines."

Masa nodded, drawing circles in the sand with a stick. "So maybe you might be . . . reluctant to believe?" He looked up.

Mr. Bellows cocked his head.

Masa dropped the stick. "Pele is . . . Listen . . . see, not everyone believes this, but . . . Pele actually exists."

I glanced at Reverend Paia. Did church people believe this kind of thing?

Reverend Paia said, "Pele is something these boys should know about, living on this island."

"Everybody already knows about Pele," Louie mumbled, lying on the sand with his eyes closed.

"Louie," Mr. Bellows said in a tone that meant Be respectful.

"Well," Masa went on, "what I know about her is that she was once a goddess, an *akua,* who was forced away from her home in Tahiti by her bad sister, Namakaokahai. Pele had to flee with her two brothers, who had shark bodies and who guided her safely to these islands."

"Maybe Fred knows them," Casey said.

"Maybe Fred's *one* of them," I added, joking.

"Who's Fred?" Mr. Bellows said.

"A shark, Dad. Out there by the island. We saw it today. Masa knows it."

Mr. Bellows turned to Masa. "This is getting stranger by the minute."

"Go on, Mr. Masa," I said.

"Well . . . when Pele got to Hawaii, she found a home up at the volcano, right above where we are now. She dug a deep pit to live in. She had many brothers and sisters, and some of them lived with her. For a long, long time she been in this area. Still now she wanders around her volcano home. People have told of running into her on a lonely road in the black of night. She might appear as an elderly woman in your headlights, or sometimes as a beautiful young girl. People who have seen her tell of how she would smile . . . then vanish."

I liked hearing about this kind of stuff, like the night marchers, even though it was scary, especially around a campfire at night in a desolate place like Halape.

"Spooky," Casey said.

"People think she's mean," Masa went on. "But she just cares about her island home. When she does get angry, she shakes the earth and the ground opens up and fire comes out . . . what we call a volcanic eruption. She has great power."

Masa turned toward the dark sea. Stars fell clear down onto the black line that marked the horizon. The air was cooler now, but still warm, and thick with salt. "In fact, right now, as we sit here," Masa went on, "Pele is at work . . . out there."

"The underwater volcano," Louie said, his eyes still closed. I thought he'd fallen asleep.

"That's right. One day it's going to pop up out of the ocean and there it will be . . . a new island. That's Pele's creation. So you can see she's also a generous akua."

"So if that white dog is her," I said, "what's she doing down here?"

Masa looked my way. "That, boy, is what has me worried. You see, it is said that when you spot Pele as a small white dog in a desolate place like Halape, or up in Kilauea or Kau . . . it usually means the volcano is going to blow."

I sat up and looked around. Tad was biting on his blue blanket. Billy peeked out from under his sweatshirt. But Mr. Bellows and Reverend Paia looked calm. "Don't worry, boys," Mr. Bellows said. "This is legend, not fact."

Masa shook his head. "Oh no, John . . . Pele is very much present, very real, and very much a part of these islands. If you see that small white dog, something's going to happen."

That night it took me hours to doze off.

Not long after I did, I bolted awake. There was something . . . I listened, then slipped out of my sleeping bag and went outside.

All was still.

I rubbed my face and took a breath. No lava oozing over the cliff. Next time someone told spooky stories maybe I should cover my head like Billy.

I shivered, but it wasn't cold. The stars—millions of them—were hard as ice. It made me feel as close to heaven as I'd ever been. I was about to go back into the shelter when I heard it.

Something was out there.

Something far, far away.

Howling dogs.

They were back.

16
NIGHT OF THE HOWLING DOGS

I found my glasses and put them on, then dug into my back-pack for my flashlight. I slipped out into the night.

The howling had stopped.

Except for the ocean whispering along the rocky shore, Halape was eerily still. Down by the cabin where the panio-los were camped, I saw the glow of a dying fire . . . and a shadow. Someone was standing in the dark like I was. Had he heard the howling, too? I looked up at the outline of the cliff. No dogs.

But I hadn't really expected to see them. What I'd heard had been too far away. They couldn't have gotten here that fast. Unless Masa was right. If the small white dog really was Pele . . . then anything was possible.

I rubbed my arms.

This place was really starting to creep me out.

I went back into the shelter and snuggled inside my sleeping bag. I took off my glasses and rubbed my eyes, trying to shake the spooky dogs out of my mind.

✛ ✛ ✛

Sometime later, the ground under me rolled.

The solid earth turned fluid. It groaned, somewhere far below.

I tore out of my sleeping bag. Struggled into my shorts. Grabbed my bouncing glasses.

I couldn't stand up.

"Casey!"

He didn't move. I crawled over and shook him. "Casey, Casey, get up! It's an earthquake!"

"Wha—?"

"An earthquake!"

He tried to sit. It was impossible.

Moments later the rolling subsided. The ground beneath us flattened and settled. We stumbled out of the shelter into the night as a horse whinnied. Zach peeked out of his tent. "What was *that*!"

"Look!" Casey said.

Down in the coconut grove two flashlight beams swept the landscape. One of them turned and headed our way. Mr. Bellows appeared out of the darkness. "You okay over here, Casey?"

"We're fine, Dad."

"Zach?"

"Yeah, fine."

"That was . . . awesome," I said. "I mean to feel the ground move like that."

"Just the earth releasing some pressure," Mr. Bellows said. "No damage done, as far as I can tell." He shined his light up toward Pu'u Kapukapu. The beam didn't reach.

"How big you think that was?" I said.

"Not big. Two-point-five, maybe three."

Somebody once told me that a magnitude of seven meant total destruction if you were anywhere near the epicenter. Had Mom and Dana felt it in Hilo? "Should we move closer to the ocean, Mr. Bellows? Get away from the cliff?"

He swept his light toward the sea. The wet rocks glistened black. I knew what he was thinking—tidal wave. Tsunami. But there was nothing out of the ordinary out there.

"No, I think you're fine where you are. But there might be a few smaller aftershocks, so be ready. That's how it usually goes."

A horse whinnied, and I heard a man soothing it, though I couldn't see them. Mr. Bellows headed over to check on Louie and Mike. A moving flashlight glowed in their tent.

The horse snorted, its hooves clacking on rock. I tapped Casey's arm. "Let's go check it out."

"I'm going back to sleep," Zach said.

The rocky ground that broke the sandy trail was treacherous in the night. It would be easy to stumble and go down hard. We had to be careful. The flashlight helped.

Masa stood with Cappy and the spooked horse. They were talking quietly. I turned off the light as we approached. "The horse all right?" I said.

"Yeah, fine. Just jumpy. This little gal is mine. Her name is Hoku."

"Star," I said.

"Right. Because of this small white patch on the forehead, see?"

I turned on my flashlight, subduing the beam by putting my hand over the lens. "Sure enough."

"How's about you boys?" Masa said.

"Fine," Casey said. "But that was scary."

"No, it wasn't," I said. "It was awesome."

Masa laughed. "Pele got a mind of her own. Every now and then she got to let you know who's boss, ah? Now you know why I was worried about that dog."

He ran one hand down Hoku's neck. In his other he held a rope that was slung over her nose and tied in what looked to me like a clove hitch. Cappy tapped Masa's arm and left to join the other paniolos, who were with the rest of the horses. The horses weren't tied up.

"How do you keep them from running away?" I asked Masa.

"Shine your light by the feet."

A short length of rope coupled Hoku's front legs together. "Ah," I said. "You handcuffed them."

Masa chuckled. "Hobbled, is what we call it . . . but handcuffed works." He slipped the rope off Hoku's nose and rubbed her neck one more time. "You go back to sleep, girl. Dream about all that sweet kikuyu grass back home."

When I looked up, the stars seemed extra bright, extra sharp, as if they'd been electrified or repowered. Maybe Pele had lured them closer.

Masa followed my gaze. Hoku nudged his arm and he cupped her nose with his hand, looking at the stars.

"You believe in ghosts, Masa?"

He scratched Hoku's chin, thinking. "Well . . . sometimes I wonder."

"About ghosts?"

"About lot of things . . . what we don't know, what we can't see."

"Like UFOs," Casey said.

"Sure," Masa said. "Can't be just us in all this," he said, opening his hand to the universe.

Casey looked up. "You really think that dog was Pele? I mean, *really*?"

Masa grunted. "I live and work in her backyard, boy. I ain't saying nothing more about her, nothing. She wants to come around as a dog, then that's fine with me. She wants to shake up the earth, no problem."

"If Pele was the white dog," I asked, "who was the black one?"

"Bodyguard," Masa said, clapping his hand on my shoulder. I smiled.

Cappy came back. "They okay, boss. I going sleep."

"Me too," Masa said. "See you boys tomorrow."

Back in the shelter I shook my sleeping bag out in case any roaches or red ants had crawled into it. I took off my glasses and rolled up my T-shirt for a pillow. It felt good to lie down. I was tired but my eyes were wide open. I forced myself to think about anything but earthquakes and howling dogs.

Just as I was about to doze off, something like rocks rattled down on the tin roof of our shelter. I yelped and stumbled out, Casey right behind me, both of us ready for another earthquake to slam us down any second.

Outside, Louie and Mike were staggering around like drunks, laughing their brains out.

"You *freaks*!" Casey yelled.

My heart was hammering so hard I thought it would pop out of my chest. "Get out of here!" I picked up a stick.

They stumbled away, holding each other up.

"What's going on?" Zach said, peeking out of his tent.

"Mike and Louie."

"Got it," Zach said, and vanished back into his tent.

Casey spat. "I *hate* them!"

"What time is it?"

He flashed his light on his watch. "Four-twenty."

Back in the shelter I rerolled my T-shirt pillow and lay back. "What a night," I mumbled, closing my eyes. Sleep finally came.

And then the world fell apart.

17
LIKE NO OTHER

First came the sound.

Somewhere far, far below. Under me. A groaning, like a stubborn nail being pulled out of wood. My eyes popped open as the earth trembled. I sat up on my elbow. My sleeping bag was jiggling. Then it jerked, leaped, and tossed me into the air. The dirt floor came up and hit me like a hammer. "Uhhhn!"

Get out! Get out!

I kicked my way out of my sleeping bag, tearing at the zipper. Broke free, tried to stand. Fell. "Casey!"

Outside, the night was black as tar. I fumbled for my flashlight, but the earth belched again and threw me up with a violence I would never have thought possible. Then it rolled under itself and sucked me into it, went down like a broken elevator.

"Caseyyy!"

It rolled back up and tossed me into the air.

I hit the ground hard.

I could see the black shadow of Casey ripping at his bag. The earth was slamming him around like a pebble in a tin can, shuddering, making a terrible noise. He freed himself and tumbled out into the night.

The world was tearing itself apart. Ripping, twisting. The whole island screamed and howled and rattled like a monstrous jackhammer . . . *Da-ka-da-ka-da-ka-da-ka!*

I could hear Casey grunting and gasping as he banged around on the hard dirt, air rushing out of him. Outside the shelter a new sound, terrifying beyond any other: the roar of an army of dump trucks dropping gravel from their beds over all of Halape. The cliff.

No, no, no! The cliff is coming down!

My glasses! My glasses! Where are my glasses!

I felt around, slapping my hand on the ground. There! I gripped them as if they were life itself. Without them I'd be nearly helpless. I put them on and thanked God they were tied to the fishing-line cord.

Casey shrieked, his voice nearly lost in all the noise.

"Casey!" I called.

I yelped as the shelter's rock walls started caving in. The tin roof clanked down, nearly hammering me on the head. I rolled out onto the sand. Casey called, but his voice was swallowed by the darkness, by the shrieking earth. "Here! Casey, over here!"

The ground slowed and shivered, straining, the popping sound of a ship pulling at its dock ropes.

Then the boulders.

Boom! Bam!

Pu'u Kapukapu was coming apart, huge chunks of cliff falling away in the darkness.

"*Casey,* we got to get to the water! The boulders!"

His shape crawled toward me.

"Flashlight!" he shouted. "Where's my—" He found it and turned it on. Its beam wobbled in his shaking hand. He dropped it, and the light bounced on the dirt, the earth now shaking like a dog with a rat. The light went out.

Boulders pounded down, their concussions vibrating through dirt, sand, and rock.

Over in the coconut grove someone screamed, and horses shrieked.

My hands trembled wildly, but I managed to stand and scramble away from the shelter with Casey. Again, the earth slammed me down. Pain stabbed my shoulder. My glasses came loose and fell off my face and would have been lost in the blackness if not for the cord.

Casey bounced up and came down hard. "*Ayii!* My knee, my knee!"

I crawled over to him. He was rolled into a ball, both hands gripping his knee, moaning. "Ow, ow, ow!"

"We got to get away from here, Casey. Can you walk?"

"Ahhh . . . it hurts!"

"We got to move. . . . The boulders—"

"I can't."

I gripped him under his arms and dragged him across the sand toward the ocean. Thundering vibrations buzzed through me as boulders slammed down from Pu'u Kapukapu and bounced toward the sea.

I looked up, remembering Zach. "Zach! *Zach!*"

A car-sized rock careened toward the sea, a giant shadow crossing the trail between our shelter and the coconut grove. The island shook, as if laughing. Earth broke under me. I lost my grip on Casey, because we were falling. The earth sucking down, down. I tried to scream but nothing came out. Casey bounced into me, and the earth tossed us back up. Somebody cried out, not far away. "Zach!" I howled. No answer.

Far below, I could hear the earth shifting into some new place, and the noise would not stop, would not stop, would not stop, the land was coming apart and it would not stop.

I heard Casey crying. I couldn't help him. I couldn't help myself. "Zach!" I shouted. "Where are you!"

More boulders tumbled toward the sea.

I covered my head with my arms. Any one of them would crush me like a bug. My throat burned with grief: we would all die. We would be smashed.

Then it stopped.

The earth rolled over and slowed. The terrifying snarl subsided and the crushing boulders bounced into new places and settled.

It was over.

The earth hissed and sighed.

All was silent.

I gasped for air and rose to my knees with my arms still shielding my head. I could feel the wetness of a bloody nose. I rubbed the blood away. My shoulder ached.

109

Soft cries whimpered in the darkness.

"Zach! Are you out there?"

Still no answer.

Casey was curled into a ball near me in the dark, his hands gripping his knee, sobbing low.

The earth gasped. It was something I could sense, not hear. Catching its breath. Pressure building. It wouldn't be long. The rattling would come back, and this time it would kill us!

"Casey," I whispered in the eerie silence. "We got to move! We got to go by the grove, by your dad. Closer to the sea."

Out of the blackness, two figures stumbled over us. Louie and Mike. Louie flicked a flashlight on.

"It's us!" I said. "Me and Casey."

"You hurt?"

"Casey's knee."

Louie crouched. "Show me."

Casey's eyes were pinched in pain.

Mike glanced at our crumbled shelter. "Ho," he whispered. "You got out just in time."

"I can't find Zach! Look for him."

Mike tried, but it was too dark. "We need another flashlight. You got one?"

"No. We lost it."

We were all in shorts and T-shirts, barefoot. My boots were probably under a pile of rocks. I'd have to dig them out.

Casey took his hand off his knee. Blood oozed between his fingers and streaked down his leg. An ugly gash across his kneecap showed the bone.

"Pretty bad," Louie said.

"Mike!" I said. "Check Zach's tent!"

Mike borrowed the flashlight and ran over to peek into Zach's tent, which still stood. "Not in here."

"Maybe he went to the grove."

Louie stood and helped Casey to his feet, then slipped an arm around his waist. "We go . . . while we can."

The four of us lurched through the dark over the sand and rocks toward the grove, Louie with Casey, Mike with the only light. How long until sunrise?

Too long.

We stopped when we felt the earth coming back to life. Dread swelled in me. No, no!

"Haw!" Mike said when way out on the horizon a flash of unworldly light lit the ocean, like some silent scream from the deep emptiness beyond.

"What was *that*?" I said.

We couldn't even guess. It wasn't stormy out there, as far as I could tell. The soundless flash made no sense.

"Keep moving," Louie said.

We were almost to the coconut grove when the earth trembled. Like before, in the center of the earth. "Here it comes," Mike said.

The land rolled up, and up, then fell, and we fell with it.

Down, down, down.

Then up.

It knocked the air out of me and I gasped.

The earth grabbed Casey from Louie's hands. Casey screamed, coming down yards away. Mike hit hard and Louie bounced like a rubber ball.

There was a huge shudder. A sigh. Then everything broke apart, sand slipping through cracks—the dirt, the rocks, and the coconut grove.

All that was around us.

Sank.

And the ocean rushed in.

18

HIGHER GROUND

We're dead, I thought as I heard the ocean churning toward us. Rumbling in, slow at first, then rising up, faster and faster.

"Pop!" Mike shouted, trying to run toward the coconut grove. He never made it.

Water rushed in. It grabbed my ankles, swirled around them, and rose higher. I tried to slog inland, but there was nowhere to go. Louie flashed his light out at the mountain of white water boiling toward us as the earth continued to sink, taking us down with it. He whipped the light back toward the cliff. Boulders flashed in the beam, tumbling down. In the eerie light, two huge monsters bounced over our shelter, crushing it, then rolled on to vanish in the oncoming sea.

"Louie!" I howled. The sea was bearing down on us like a garbage truck.

He whipped the light back.

The wall of water came at us head-on, a mountain in the puny beam of light. We stumbled back, falling over rocks we couldn't see. Going down, struggling to stand. Louie heaved Casey up onto his shoulders and staggered inland. He tried to hang on to the flashlight, but it was lost in the ocean rushing around our waists. The light glowed underwater and went out as it sank.

The ocean knocked me off my feet. I flailed inland, my glasses tight in my fist. I would never let them go. No matter what.

I gasped a last breath . . . and went under.

The water dragged me over rocks and bushes with sharp branches. Tumbling, tumbling. It tossed me up for one more merciful gulp of air, then pulled me down again and carried me back, back, back, back toward the cliff.

Then it slowed and sucked me the other way, out to sea, so deep now that I felt nothing, no bushes, no rocks.

My foot hit something once—a branch, a body—then whatever it was vanished and I spun in a watery void, not knowing up from down, spinning, spinning, spinning in a bubbly mass.

Air!

Need air!

I felt the horror of deep water sucking me down.

Breathe!

Can't.

Surge. Moving back. Going inland.

Gagging.

Rolling, tumbling.

Drowning.

Back over land. Upside-down, dragged through bushes, branches. Banged, scratched, ripped.

Stuck.

Caught in something; a bush.

Got to get out!

Need . . . air. . . .

Need . . .

No. . . .

Let go. . . . Let go.

Let . . . go. . . .

It's over.

Easy.

Glasses . . . Don't need them. . . . Don't need anything. . . . Easy . . . I opened my hand and let my glasses drift away, the cord unraveling. Gone.

Mom . . . Dad . . .

In that moment the wave subsided.

Stars.

I was out! I coughed and gasped and heaved in great gulps of air as the angry ocean withdrew and left me twisted in a mess of sharp branches.

My eyes flooded.

Alive. I'm alive.

I lay in the bush, gasping and tangled. I sucked in air, my heart pounding. Slowly, I struggled free.

Where was I?

Farther in, that was for sure. But how far?

My glasses! Why did I let them go?

I felt around the wet ground in the dark. You let them go because you were dead, remember? There was no reason for you to keep them. You didn't need them anymore.

Yes, yes.

I was dead.

I would never forget that.

Being dead. Being nothing. How easy it was to be nothing. A sob broke out of me. I sagged and folded on a wet patch of sand. Then I popped up, remembering I wasn't alone.

"Casey!" I croaked. My throat was raw. It hurt to call out. I had to. "Louie, Mike! Where are you?"

"Over . . . here . . ."

I turned but saw nothing. "Where?"

A shadow appeared. "Louie?"

The stars were bright and clear beyond, reflected on a calming sea that seemed to know nothing of what had just happened. "Come," Louie said, grabbing my hand and pulling me to my feet.

"My glasses," I said. "I dropped them."

"We find um later. Too dark now. We got to go higher."

"Where's Mike?"

"I don't know. Come, walk."

There was a groan.

I saw movement, someone limping. "That you, Mike?" Louie said.

It was. "I have to find Pop." He walked past, zombielike, back into the darkness.

Farther up someone screamed, panicking. Billy or Tad. Then the screaming stopped and I heard voices.

"Help me . . . someone . . . anyone."

I whipped around.

Casey was sprawled in a patch of mud, moaning. I knelt down. His knee still bled. More blood oozed from a new cut on his cheek.

Louie knelt beside me. " 'S'okay, brah. We help you."

We looked up when a paniolo appeared out of the darkness. Then another. In the light of the stars I saw that one was Masa. His wet clothes clung to him and a dark line of blood dripped from his hair to his jaw. "You boys all right?"

"We okay," Louie said, somehow not stunned speechless like me. "Casey got a cut knee. The rest of us drank some salt water. You seen Mr. Bellows and the Reveren'?"

"Nobody but you," Masa said. "Come. We climb higher now. Talk later."

"But the guys in the grove," I said, finding my voice.

"The grove is gone."

Louie and I glanced back into the darkness. I couldn't see a thing. "Gone?"

Masa tugged my shoulder. "Hurry. Carry this boy before more water comes."

We lifted Casey to his feet. He was heavy; his head hung. He moaned. Masa and I got on either side of him.

"Ready?" Masa said.

"Got him."

We started uphill, slowly picking our way over rocks we

couldn't see. My glasses wouldn't have helped even if I'd had them.

"Go," Louie said. "I catch up." He headed back toward where the grove had been.

"Boy!" Masa said. "Too dangerous down there!"

But Louie was already gone.

19
A WATERY
GRAVE

"Louie, wait!" I called. "Masa, can you take Casey by yourself?"

"You don't understa—"

"Please, Masa—Zach and Mr. Bellows and some others might be down there. We got to help them."

Uphill the screaming started again.

Casey moaned.

"Go," Masa said, taking all of Casey's weight. "Come back quick. Don't stay down there."

"If we hear a wave we'll run for it."

"Find Dad," Casey squeaked.

"I'll find him, Case. Don't worry. If he's there we'll bring him up to you." I squinted, barely making Louie out. "Louie, wait!"

"Go back!" he called. "You can't see, remember? You need glasses."

"All the same in the dark," I mumbled to myself, stumbling ahead. Louie waited. "Where we going?" I said.

"We know when we get there."

I couldn't see two feet in front of me. The ocean was quiet, but my mind raced with thoughts of gagging on salt water, being held under, being gone, being nothing. Dead.

We stopped. Louie looked around.

"Where are we?" I said.

"Hard to tell. Different now. Keep going."

I tested each step, afraid I might break an ankle or fall into some sharp crevice. My face and arms started stinging. I ran my hand over my cheek. Cuts, scratches, lumps everywhere.

Louie stopped and called out. "Anybody hear me?"

"Down here."

The voice was weak.

We headed toward it.

"Keep talking," Louie said. "I can't see you."

"I'm in the crack."

"It's Reverend Paia! *Reverend*!" I called.

"Dylan?"

"Me and Louie, we're coming."

I squinted into the dark. Louie crouched next to me. I couldn't believe the crack hadn't caved in. Reverend Paia's white shirt was a faint gray in the black hole. "There," I whispered.

"Mike," Reverend Paia said. "Is he—"

"He's fine," Louie said. "He went higher up looking for you."

"Thank God, thank . . . God."

We inched down the trail toward him. "You hurt, Reveren'?" Louie said.

"My arm . . . it's broken."

"Hang on. We almost there."

Louie and I crept closer, our hands following the wall of rock. Louie stumbled, and I fell over him. He'd hit something lying on the trail. We both staggered to our feet.

"What is it?" I said.

"Dead horse," Reverend Paia said. "Sorry, I forgot it was there."

We stepped around it.

Reverend Paia wasn't alone. The murky shape of someone lay in his arms. Louie and I crouched down. "Sam?" I said.

"Tad. He swallowed a lot of ocean, but he's alive."

I stood ankle-deep at the edge of the warm brackish water. The rocks under my feet were slippery with moss. The crack was as black as black could get.

"Anybody else down here?"

"I don't think so. We need a flashlight."

"Lost mines in the wave," Louie said.

Wave. What if we were in here and another one came? The thought made my scalp tingle. "We got to get out of here!"

"Can you stand, Reveren'?" Louie said.

"We'll see. Help me with Tad."

I knelt in the water and took Tad, his head resting on my

121

shoulder. He was out cold, or asleep. I tried to stand and staggered under his weight.

"Gimme him," Louie said. "You help the Reveren'." Louie lifted Tad and carried him back up the trail.

"Give me your hand, Reverend." He gasped, and struggled to his feet. He grabbed my shoulder with his good arm. The other hung loosely at his side.

"You hurt anywhere else, sir?" I said.

"All I know for sure is that I'm breathing, son. But I can walk . . . if we go slow."

We staggered up the trail, Reverend Paia clinging to my shoulder. He was heavy. Water soaked his clothes. His skin felt clammy and he smelled like fish and seaweed. We skirted the dead horse.

Louie waited with Tad at the top.

Slowly, we made our way uphill toward where Masa and Casey had gone, and, I hoped, Mike. They had a light up there. I could see a dull glow. Reverend Paia's arm flopped around like an old hose, but he kept moving, gasping when he tripped. Tad started mumbling. A good sign.

Mike hurried down to help. "Pop!" he called.

"Boy, am I glad to see you, son." Reverend Paia winced when Mike hugged him. "Easy, Mike . . . my arm's—"

"Sorry, sorry . . . I should have—"

"Help me walk. I don't want to trip."

"Yeah, Pop, I got you." We continued up the hill.

"We found them in the crack," I said.

"Where's my dad?" Casey asked when we reached the others. "Didn't you see him?"

What could I say?

"Dad!" Casey shouted, and turned to head down the hill. He gasped at the pain in his knee.

Louie grabbed him by the shoulders. "Listen to me. . . . We going back right now, soon as we find these two someplace to sit. We won't stop looking, ah? We find him."

The only light came from a single flashlight. They'd set it on the rocks in a way that illuminated as much ground as possible. Masa, Cappy, Billy, and two other paniolos were spread out on a flat patch of dirt. Billy was sobbing.

Mike groped around until he found a place for his dad to sit. Louie eased Tad down onto a flat patch of ground and knelt beside him. "How you feeling, little man?"

"My head . . . it hurts."

"You seen some action."

Billy shrieked and Louie looked up. Masa hurried over to Billy. " 'S'okay, boy. You safe now." He pulled Billy close and glanced over at us. "Terrified."

Louie turned back to Tad.

I looked out into the darkness. Other than the one flashlight, the stars were all the light we had until sunrise. It wasn't far off. Zach, Sam, Mr. Bellows, and one paniolo—where were they?

Louie appeared at my side. "We go," he said, almost in a whisper.

Masa patted Billy's shoulder and stood. He came over. "Too dark now. Wait for morning, then go."

"Can't," Louie said. "No time to waste."

Louie was right. What if one of them was barely hanging on and needed help right now? Sunrise might be too late. "We'll be back soon," I said.

"Go," Masa said, knowing we had no choice. "Watch for Lenny. He's my cousin."

"We find him," Louie said. "Thanks for helping us."

"I'm going, too," Casey said, hopping up. He'd wrapped his knee in his T-shirt. But he still couldn't walk.

"Not with that leg," I said.

"You can't stop me!"

"Case," I said. "Me and Louie can move faster than you, and cover more ground. Let us find him. They need you here."

Casey knew I was right. He limped over to a rock and sat with his head in his hands. I thought of Dad and how I'd feel if I were in Casey's place. Nothing would stop me from looking.

"Take this," Masa said, holding up a small flashlight. "Billy had it." He handed it to Louie, who turned it on. The beam was faint. He flicked it off and stuck it in his back pocket. "Just use um when we need um."

We groped our way downhill, Louie in front.

My shorts and shirt were clammy in the morning air. I would have given anything for dry clothes and boots. It wasn't easy walking barefoot over the rocks.

Any trail that had been there before was gone now. The landscape had been rearranged. There was nothing to follow. And it was dark. But for me it was almost better that way. In the light of day it would be harder to see with no glasses. But now I could see just as well as Louie. My feet were my eyes.

Down, down, down, back toward an ocean so quiet you'd have thought nothing had happened. Starlight reflected off its silky flat surface.

"Hold it," Louie said, stopping. He flicked the flashlight's weak beam on and swept it over the ground around his feet. He squatted.

"What is it?"

"These yours?" he said, dangling my slightly twisted glasses from the fishing line, now attached to only one stem.

I grabbed them. "I can't believe you found them!"

"Stars reflected off the glass."

"Amazing."

The metal frames were bent and one lens was cracked. But the other one was still good. I bent the frames back, retied the fishing line to one stem, and put them on. They didn't help much. Too dark. So I let them hang around my neck. When the sun came up it would make all the difference in the world to have them.

"Thanks, Louie," I said. "Thanks."

He stood. "I hope we not looking for bodies."

"Mr. Bellows!" I called.

Silence.

We both yelled, "Sam! Zach! Lenny! Anybody!"

Nothing.

The sea had moved inland. I could see that now in the faint illumination of the stars. The coast as we knew it no longer existed. Never, not in my whole life, would I forget that sinking ground: going down, going under, being swallowed by the earth and the ocean at the same time.

"Sit," Louie said.

"Here?"

"Let it get little bit more light. We might pass right by somebody. Look, sun coming up soon."

The black sky was turning to deep purple. The ocean horizon cut across the east, sharp as a razor. It would be a cloudless sunrise.

We peered into the new morning, looking toward the sea and the grove where Mr. Bellows and the younger guys had set up their campsite. More and more, I became aware of my aching body, the stinging cuts and scratches, the salt crystals that inflamed them. Sitting still and thinking about the pain made it worse. I felt a large lump on the back of my head. No blood, though.

Memories came and went. Falling, sinking. Boulders. Ocean. Gagging.

Drowning.

Stars faded as dawn light grew. Shapes started to emerge. I squinted into the inky distance, trying to make out the camp in the grove. What looked like coconut trees began to appear. Black silhouettes against the lightening sea. Yes, those were the . . . the coconut trees.

I stopped breathing.

"My God," Louie whispered.

The trees were rising out of the ocean.

20
A HUMAN HEAD

The palm fronds were just as full as on any other day, healthy and green. But now they sprouted from the sea.

Had this really happened?

We sat stunned in the growing light. The crack, too, was oddly out of place, closer to the ocean. The shelters that weren't too close to the sea were piles of crushed rock, their gnarled and twisted roofing sprawled farther inland where the ocean had tossed them.

Louie tapped my arm. He stood and nodded toward a pool of water at the edge of the sea.

I creaked up and squinted. There was something there, floating. I put on my broken glasses. The cracked lens made the vision in my left eye weird. But I could see.

We headed down.

127

My stomach roiled in fear. The ocean repelled me, like a reverse magnet. I wanted to go the other way, go higher, then higher again . . . not closer. Another wave would kill me. I knew that without question. Next time I'd die for real.

Stop! Don't think. You got to find people.

I was beginning to believe that Louie had more guts than the rest of us put together. Nothing seemed to scare him, not broken arms, not a dead horse, not sinking land, not killer waves. It was as if he'd steeled himself against anything the world could throw at him. He was made of something I wasn't.

"Louie, wait up!"

He went faster and faster, leaping from rock to rock. I could hardly keep up. Sharp rocks stabbed my bare feet. I searched for smooth places to step. I'd be no good if I got cut.

I gasped and staggered to a stop when I saw what was floating in the pool of water. "That's a—"

Louie waded out to it.

A human head.

I felt sick.

"Come!" Louie called back to me.

I stumbled closer, the pain in my feet forgotten.

It was Lenny's head.

It spoke. "I'm stuck. . . . My legs broken . . . both of them."

A small wave rolled over him, submerging him. He sputtered and coughed when it passed, the water up to his chin.

Louie slipped on the uneven bottom, falling, getting back up. I jumped into the water and slogged closer, my fear of the ocean gone. All that mattered was that Lenny was alive! The tide was coming in and we had to get him out.

"Rocks on my legs," he said, wincing.

Louie fell to his knees, feeling underwater. I knelt behind Lenny and propped his head up in my hands. His hair was long and fell into his eyes. I swept it away so he could see. He was a young guy, maybe twenty-five.

"Ai-yah!" he yelped, as Louie began lifting rocks away.

"Sorry. Can you move now?" Louie said.

Lenny shook his head. "Only . . . this one arm. I . . . I broke up too bad."

Louie moved all the rocks away and glanced at me. "Get on the other side. We going lift him and carry him out. How's the pain, Lenny? Can you take it?"

Lenny touched a curved scar on his chin. "When I was seventeen a bull wen' kick out my teeth and broke my jaw."

"Guess that's a yes," I said. I moved around to his side. "Okay, I got him."

Louie reached under Lenny. He smiled at him before we lifted. "Nice to meet you, Lenny. You ready?"

Lenny hooked his good arm around my neck and squeezed his eyes shut. "Go."

He gasped when we lifted him, the heavy water in his clothes tugging him back. His broken arm flopped, and Louie laid it across his chest. The break was just above his elbow, the bone trying to poke out of the skin. His legs dangled like dead eels. He was missing one boot.

Careful not to slip and fall, we moved Lenny up out of the water, carried him to a patch of sand and set him down. "I thought my time was up," he said, and squeezed his eyes shut.

Louie turned to look up toward the others. It was lighter now, and we could see them clearly. Masa was watching us.

Could he see that we'd found Lenny? I waved him down. He raised a hand and turned to get help.

"All the time I was in the water I could hear you folks up there," Lenny said.

"We going carry you, Lenny," Louie said. "Might hurt little bit."

Lenny nodded.

I looked over my shoulder.

Masa, Cappy, and Mike were easing their way down over the uneven ground.

"Wait," I said. "Help is on the way."

Louie lifted his chin toward me. "That four-eyed ugly is Dylan, Lenny. I'm Louie."

"Louie . . . like the guy writes the westerns."

"Westerns?"

A horse whinnied.

Hearing the horse, Lenny tried to get up, forgetting his broken bones. "Ahhh . . . ahhh!"

"The horses are fine," Louie said. "I can see three of them right now."

"One was in the crack," I said. "Dead."

"Ahh . . . shoot," Lenny said.

Louie gave me a look and shook his head: Shut up.

"Who is it?" Masa called, almost down to us.

I looked up. "Lenny! It's Lenny."

Masa crouched and put his hand on Lenny's shoulder. "What kind of mess you got yourself in now, cousin?"

Lenny grinned. "Couple broken bones, is all."

"Thank goodness."

Cappy and Mike leaned in over Masa. Lenny said, "That's

130

the first time I ever heard anyone say thank goodness for broken bones, boss." He tried to laugh. It hurt, so he stopped. His eyes were rimmed with red.

"Pele must be angry with you," Masa said. "What you did to make her mad?"

"Nothing, boss. . . . Mistaken identity."

Masa shook his head.

Lenny lifted his one good arm. "This is all I got left, but I be back on my horse quick as a wink."

"Sure you will," Masa said, ruffling Lenny's hair.

In the growing light I could see that each of us was covered with cuts, bruises, and scratches. It was as if we'd been attacked by a Weedwacker. I checked my arms and legs. Nothing too bad. The lump on my head didn't hurt.

I looked up to judge the distance we would have to carry Lenny. Reverend Paia was looking down, watching us. His arm was in a homemade sling. "Where's Casey?" I said to Masa. "I don't see him up there."

Masa frowned. "Went looking for his daddy."

"When?"

"It was still dark."

"But his knee."

"He found a stick to use like a cane."

I stood and studied the coast in both directions. "There he is." I could see him up the coast, a small figure near where Tad had hidden from the wasps.

Just then, there was another howl. The dogs! Closer this time.

"It's them," Masa said, looking up.

I scanned the landscape. No dogs.

Masa, still squatting with Lenny, pointed his chin toward where the howling had come from. "Go," he said. "We take Lenny up."

"Go where?" I said.

"The dogs. They calling."

"What?"

"Go!"

I looked down the coast. It was as empty of life as the moon. "Masa," I said. "There's nothing there."

He stood and squinted into the distance. "You wrong, boy. Those dogs howling about something new."

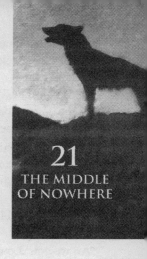

21
THE MIDDLE OF NOWHERE

Louie looked out at the ocean, studying it closely.

"You thinking what I'm thinking?" Masa said.

Louie nodded.

"What?" I said.

Louie frowned, his lips tight. "Maybe the others got sucked out to sea. . . . Maybe the ocean taking them south. . . . Maybe they drowned."

Sharks jumped into my mind . . . and the memory of sinking into the silent black depths.

Louie started out, heading in the direction of the howling. It had stopped, but the sound still lingered in my mind. I couldn't move. This nightmare was getting all too real. I leaned over and put my hands on my knees, dizzy.

"Go slow," Masa said, nudging me toward Louie.

I nodded, still bent over.

The dizziness settled. I stood. Don't think, just do it. I headed after Louie.

The round rocks were no problem, but the jagged ones slowed me down. Louie waited, looking back.

"Two things could have happened," he said when I caught up. "They got buried under the rocks or sucked out to sea. Maybe they drowned. But if they got sucked out, the current would drag them that way."

He gazed south.

I looked at the bleak coast. It grew hazy in the far distance.

"All we got," Louie said.

I nodded. We moved on.

Camping gear bobbed in the small waves along the rocky shore—half-submerged sleeping bags, ground pads and air mattresses, food containers, clothes, tangled tents. It would take forever to collect all that stuff. But who cared?

Louie held up a hand. Just offshore, a dead horse was stuck on the rocks. Its ballooned belly was all we could see. Small waves bobbled it. "There's the last one."

"Man, I hate to see that," I said, turning away.

Louie watched the water.

"Let's go," I said. "I don't want to look at that horse."

"Yeah, fine. Just checking the current."

We hiked on over the slippery rocks and boulders along the edge of the sea. "Look at all the dead fish," I said. They were everywhere, dragged inland and left high and dry.

I glanced back as we started around the point. Masa and

Lenny had made it back to the others higher up. From where we were, they were just smudges of color.

Around the point and farther on, the low coast turned into cliffs, way down where the island grew fuzzy. If we had to go that far, carrying someone back would be almost impossible. And if they'd gone as far as the cliffs, we'd never be able to get down to them and pull them out.

The sun now was a fireball climbing the sky. The ocean was quiet. I could hardly believe it had just tried to kill us.

"How far should we go?" I said. "A half hour?"

Louie squinted at the heat waves already rising off the rocks in the distance. "Whatever it takes. I'd walk around this island six times to find them."

I flinched. I would, too. So why'd I say a half hour?

"Yeah," I said, looking away. "But . . . but what if they're not in the water? What if they got buried in the landslide? Or what if they're trapped inside the . . . the crack? Way in the back?"

"We were there. We didn't see them."

"It was dark."

Louie squatted, concentrating. "Okay . . . we go down the coast for thirty minutes. We don't find anything, one of us goes back to check the crack."

"Good. Let's do it."

The sun's heat was growing stronger by the minute. But Louie kept on going, hopping from rock to rock. *I'd walk around this island six times to find them.* Why had that thought lived in Louie's mind and not mine?

Mr. Bellows, Zach, Sam! Where are you!

I squeezed shut the eye behind the cracked lens and tried to keep up. It was hard; you need two eyes to get three dimensions. Using only one eye left my vision flat . . . which wasn't good for jumping rocks. But it was better than adding the distortion of the cracked lens.

Ten minutes went by.

Down close to the ocean, the rocks had been smoothed by the sea and were easier on my feet.

Fifteen minutes.

Twenty.

"Dylan!" Louie pointed out to sea.

Something was out there, way out. Looked like two bodies hanging over an air mattress. "Yeah! *Yeah!*"

"Looks like Mr. Bellows . . . and Sam, maybe. I don't think that's Zach."

We scrambled down to the water, black crabs scattering into the cracks as we approached.

I shaded my eyes. "Are they moving?"

"No."

"We got to get out to them."

"I can't . . . I can't swim that far."

I tried to judge the distance. Looked like half a mile. Maybe more, and maybe I couldn't swim that far, either. And what about sharks? If we'd seen one, there could be more . . . maybe lots more.

"Never been a good swimmer," Louie said, bunching his lips. For the first time I noticed that his shark's tooth and silver skull were missing.

I looked out to sea. It would be five times farther than I'd ever gone before, at least.

But there was no other choice. The cliffs were not that far away, and the current was taking them south. Another few miles of drifting would make it impossible for us to get to them. The cliffs were too high. There'd be no way to bring them up. This was our only chance.

I handed Louie my glasses and ripped off my T-shirt, then moved onto a rock that jutted out over a spot where the water was deep enough to jump. "Keep your eyes on us," I said.

"I follow you on the rocks."

The ocean was warm. It stung my cuts, but it felt good to swim, easier than crabbing over the boulders onshore.

"Haole!" Louie called. I turned back. "You can do it!"

I hoped he was right.

I started too fast. In minutes my heart was pounding. My arms were weakening. Slow down. Pace yourself.

I caught glimpses of the air mattress. It was blue . . . and so far away . . . too far.

Swim. Don't think about it. Keep moving.

Closer, closer.

I stopped to rest, my legs dangling, drifting, moving just enough to keep my head up. Back on shore I could see Louie moving slowly down the coast to keep pace with the barely noticeable current. "Thank you for being so peaceful today," I whispered to the ocean.

I swam on.

And on.

Glancing up, making sure I was still aiming for them.

Keep moving. . . . Keep—

When I saw it, I gasped and sank. I gagged on swallowed

ocean, came back up coughing, wiping water from my eyes and frantic to be sure I'd seen what I thought I had. . . . There!

A fin.

Fear slammed into me. A lone shark was circling Sam and Mr. Bellows. How could I get to them now? Dread burst inside me. I sank again and came up gasping.

The fin turned and headed toward me. I squeaked out a cry of shock and turned wildly to swim back toward the island.

Too far.

I squeezed my eyes shut and pulled my feet up into a ball. And sank. Kicked and rose again, breathing fear and salt water.

The fin came toward me.

I could see the ripples it made as it cut the water, coming closer and closer.

"Dad!"

I thought I saw Mr. Bellows look up.

The shark was almost on me.

Close, so close.

The same eerie stillness washed over me that I'd felt when I'd believed the rushing sea had killed me. Rest. No need to panic now. It's over.

Let go.

I watched death approach.

But the fin slipped past, not five feet away, and I could see the dark, puckered hole. It circled me once. And vanished.

Poof!

138

Went under. Gone.

All that was left was a vast ocean and a blue air mattress.

"Mr. Bellows!"

He peeked up, then sagged back down.

I swam as fast as I could, wanting to climb up on that air mattress with them, get out of the water.

"Mr. Bellows!"

Was he hurt? Had the shark attacked him? Where was it now? I swirled around, searching for it. Sank and opened my eyes to an underwater emptiness that glowed. Deep blue radiated up in rays, as if there were a light at the bottom, a thousand fathoms down.

I came up gasping and wiped the water from my face. Looking back, I could barely see Louie, now squatting on the rocks looking out at us.

I started swimming again.

Not far. Keep going, don't stop now.

So tired.

Stay up, kick.

My arms slapped the water. Desperate strokes.

My hand hit something. I yanked it back and looked up. Blue.

Blue!

Mr. Bellows lifted his head. Blood streaked down his face.

"Mr. Bel—"

I sank, sputtering. My arms were weak, almost useless.

Mr. Bellows reached out and grabbed my hand. His arm was ripped with cuts. *Semper Fidelis* was all sliced up.

I clung to his hand, too tired to speak.

"Thank God," Mr. Bellows croaked, his voice raspy.

"Me and . . . Louie . . . we . . ."

My arms trembled. I rested on the edge of the air mattress. The current slowly carried us south.

Suddenly I looked up. "Did you get bit . . . by a shark?"

"No . . . but it was here," he said weakly.

"Can you kick, Mr. Bellows? We have to make it back."

"I can try," he whispered.

"Is Sam . . ."

"Weak . . . The heat . . . Casey . . . is—"

"He's okay. . . . We moved higher up. . . . He has a cut knee."

He closed his eyes and laid his head on his arm.

I was so tired I could hardly move. But I had to. The current was dragging us away. I gulped air, deeply. Searched for strength.

"Mr. Bellows, we have to move."

We started kicking. Slowly moving toward an island that now seemed impossibly far away.

I gave it more.

The easy current carried us gently, luring us into the great emptiness of the Pacific Ocean, where there would be nothing but weeks or months of empty sea. No one would ever find us. We'd be nearly invisible specks.

Louie stood and followed along the shore as we slowly drifted south.

Kick!

It took hours. Or maybe it was only one. Mr. Bellows stopped kicking soon after we'd started. He seemed dazed.

But I kept going, whispering, "Kick . . . kick . . . kick." Like a clock. My mind locked. Kick, kick.

I lifted my head at the sound of a voice. Faint, but clear. "Push it! Push! You almost here!"

I looked up and saw him waving from shore. "You can do it!" He jumped down into a cove. There was a small coral beach. I aimed for it.

Louie waded out as far as he could. The bottom fell away quickly. There were no shallows on the island, anywhere. It was an undersea mountaintop.

"Mr. Bellows," I said. "We're almost there."

He raised his head. The sight of land seemed to revive him. He struggled to kick. We surged ahead, and when we got close to the coral beach, he let go and tried to swim. Louie grabbed him. Mr. Bellows looked back.

"Go," I said. "I got Sam."

Louie helped Mr. Bellows climb up to dry rock. Mr. Bellows wore only a white T-shirt and his boxer shorts. Sam was shirtless, in a pair of white skivvies.

Louie found a place for Mr. Bellows to sit, then dropped back down to pull me, Sam, and the air mattress in. "Here," he said, handing me my glasses. I took them in my fist, my spent arms shaking. I put my head down on the air mattress. "I'm so tired."

"Sleep later. Look."

I peeked up.

Sam was stirring. He moaned. "Sammy," Louie said, and Sam tried to raise his head. "You safe now. . . . We going help you out. . . . You ready?"

Sam nodded.

I was so relieved I dropped my head back onto the air mattress. Sam was doing better than he'd looked.

"Wake up," Louie said, shaking my arm.

I found my footing on the sharp coral beach. Louie and I each took one of Sam's arms and helped him out of the water. His eyes were rimmed red and swollen. Blood oozed in small tears from his cuts. The ocean hadn't let them dry out. But there were no deep gashes, and no broken bones, as far as I could tell. We climbed up to dry rock and let him lie down.

I felt his skin. Hot, clammy.

Louie knelt and put his ear to Sam's chest. "Fast heartbeat. We got to find some shade, cool him down."

I looked up, searching. Shade wasn't something we were going to find.

"We make it," Louie said, reading my thoughts.

"Heatstroke?"

"Prob'ly . . . or close."

We laid Sam down on the flattest rocks we could find. Louie pulled his T-shirt off and took it down to soak in the ocean. He wrung the water out, brought the shirt back, and folded it over Sam's forehead. "Wet your shirt," he said. "It's over there." I grabbed it, soaked it, and tossed it up to Louie.

Shade . . . anyplace out of the sun.

But there was no such place.

Mr. Bellows crawled over and sat next to Sam. "We got dragged out to sea in the second wave. We were—" He stopped suddenly and pointed. "Grab that air mattress. Don't let it get away."

I climbed down and waded out, the hungry sea already tugging it from the shore.

Mr. Bellows took it from me. "This saved our lives . . .

and we can use it as a shelter." He stood it on its side, blocking Sam from the blazing sun. Hot shade flooded over him. Scratches like spiderwebs crisscrossed his back and stomach, his arms, legs, and face. Sam had taken a beating. We all had.

"Thank you," Mr. Bellows said. "Both of you . . . for finding us."

"It was Louie. He's the one."

"You swam out," Louie said. "I couldn't." He nodded toward the sea. "Took guts."

I turned and saw the shark fin.

"Was following you."

"I . . . I thought it was gone."

Louie stood and squinted. "Same one we saw before. . . . Look. . . . See the bullet hole?"

"Masa was right," I whispered.

Mr. Bellows looked toward the point, Halape just beyond. He was dazed, but he could still reason. "The rest of the boys . . . is anyone missing?"

"Only Zach," Louie said. "Maybe Casey found him by now. He went looking for you."

"Reverend Paia has a broken arm," I added. "And Lenny has a broken arm and two broken legs . . . but we're all still alive. It's only Zach we don't know about."

"We have to find him," Mr. Bellows said. Worry lines crowded his eyes. "I—"

"Hey," Louie said gently. "We going do that. Right now we got to get you and Sam out of the sun."

Mr. Bellows squinted up. He touched a cut on his forehead and winced. Blood was starting to cake around it.

"It doesn't look too bad," I said.

"Stings like the devil."

"Salt," Louie said.

Mr. Bellows pushed himself to his feet. He wobbled and reached out to steady himself, grabbing Louie's shoulder.

I removed the wet T-shirts and helped Sam stand. I wasn't sure he could walk.

Mr. Bellows let the air out of the mattress and folded it, then tucked it under his arm. "Let's go back to camp, boys."

What camp? I thought.

I climbed back down to the water and resoaked the shirts but didn't squeeze them out. The wetter the better. I took them back and draped one over Sam's head and the other around his neck.

I lifted my chin for Louie to grab Sam's other arm. Together, we slowly headed back the way we'd come.

Sam could walk, but not very well. He wasn't looking so good. I glanced at Louie.

He shook his head and scanned the rocks, searching for the next safe step. And the next one after that.

22

THE ONLY OPTION

Ten minutes later we stopped to rest. Sam could barely put one foot in front of the other. We had to struggle to keep him upright. He started moaning, his eyes rolling back into his head.

"He needs to lie down," Mr. Bellows said.

We eased Sam onto the smoothest section of lava we could find. He sat and blinked, his eyes glazed and half-open.

Mr. Bellows knelt next to him.

"Sam . . . can you hear me?"

He didn't respond.

"Sam?"

Louie and I glanced at each other. "Make him some shade," Louie said. "Use the shirts. I going get help."

He headed out, leaping the rocks like a mountain goat. I'd never seen him move so fast.

"Bring water!" I yelled.

Sam mumbled, then groaned. I put the T-shirts neck to neck and tied the sleeves together to make a sun shield. I shifted so I stood between Sam and the sun, holding the shirts up to make shade. With only skivvies on, his skin was almost completely exposed. I could put one of the T-shirts on him, but that would reduce the amount of shade I could make. There wasn't enough as it was.

"Mr. Bellows?"

He looked up. His eyes were starting to puff and swell.

"You feel up to holding this over Sam while I go look for some sticks to make a tent out of these shirts?"

Mr. Bellows struggled up. I gave him the shirts. "You feeling all right, Mr. Bellows?"

"Fine, Dylan, fine."

I studied him a moment. He was anything but fine. I headed out to hunt for sticks, turning back once. I felt bad for Mr. Bellows. He was hurting.

Higher up I found four surf-rounded pieces of driftwood. I could use them as posts. Louie, now, wasn't far from the point. I could still see him. It would be close to an hour before he got back.

I hurried back to Sam and Mr. Bellows.

Sam had fallen asleep, curled up at the edge of a crevice. Mr. Bellows sat with his head in his hands. The T-shirts were on the rocks, drying quickly in the sun. I looked into the crevice. There was water at the bottom, a pool maybe five inches deep. I climbed down and put my foot into it. Warm. But it was wet. Could I get Sam down here?

I looked up at Mr. Bellows and raked my brain, trying to remember what the Scout handbook said about heatstroke. Rapid pulse . . . noisy breathing . . . yeah, that . . . and hot skin. But in this sun everything was hot.

I managed to ease Sam down into the crevice and sat him in the shallow pool of water. I put my ear to his back. His breathing sounded normal. Not fast, not scratchy. I leaned him back against the wall of the crevice.

I climbed out and secured the shirts to the four pieces of driftwood and jammed the sticks into cracks between the rocks above the crevice. They made a roof, shading Sam's head and chest.

I scowled at my pitiful shelter. It barely made a dent in the relentless heat, the shade of a spindly weed in a desert.

I turned back to Mr. Bellows, still with his head down. "Mr. Bellows," I said softly.

He looked up, then put his head back in his hands. The folded air mattress lay in the sun next to him.

The air mattress!

Where is my *brain*!

I jumped up and hopped inland, found more sticks and made a lean-to, propping up the limp air mattress by poking the sticks through the brass rope rings at the corners. "Crawl under this, Mr. Bellows."

He moved slowly, mumbling.

I stood and looked back toward the point. Louie was around the bend now. Out of sight. The barren coast shimmered in the heat, the rocks wobbling in my vision like disturbed reflections in a pool of water. Hurry, Louie, hurry.

147

I swept my gaze over the landscape behind me, hoping to spot something else I could use to make shade. What else should I be doing? I should have taken my first-aid merit badge more seriously.

I spotted something . . . a piece of cardboard? "I'll be right back, Mr. Bellows."

My feet had stopped hurting. I had a few cuts, but the soles of my feet were tougher. Moving over the uneven rocks had gotten easier. Which was good, because my cracked glasses weren't helping much. Busted up as I was, it felt good to move like that, feeling the motion, the freedom.

What I'd spotted wasn't cardboard. It was a large warped piece of plywood, maybe four feet square.

I lifted it and carried it over my head, moving fast. "Mr. Bellows," I called. "Look what I found!"

He didn't move.

I searched for more depressions, crevices like Sam was in. Holes with water in them. I found one not too far from Sam's. It was big enough. "Mr. Bellows . . . if you get down between these rocks I can put a better roof over you."

Slowly, he looked up.

"This way," I said, waving him over.

He crawled out from under the air mattress and made his way to the hole. "Get down in here," I said. "I can make better shade for you."

He eased down into the warm pool. Water had been trapped there. The whole coast must have been hit with the giant waves.

"That's good, Mr. Bellows."

I set the plywood over him, then collected rocks and

raised it higher by making stacks under the corners. I took down his old air-mattress shelter and carried it over to make more shade for Sam. It helped.

Sam slept; at least, I hoped it was sleep, not some kind of heat coma. I had to get some water into him. "Come on, Louie," I whispered, looking up. Would there even be any water? Was the catchment still standing? I hadn't noticed.

I took the T-shirts down to the ocean and soaked them, then hurried back and untied the sleeves. I placed one shirt over Sam's head and stretched the other across his back. I doubted they were doing very much to cool him down. But even a little was something. The sun had shifted. I hadn't realized until that moment just how fast it moved. I adjusted the air mattress and slab of plywood to maintain the shade. It was all I could do.

The sun was frying my back; I could almost hear the skin sizzling. Not good. I got up and searched for another watery hole, found one closer to the ocean, and scrunched down into it. Water, but no shade. The sun was too high. I splashed warm liquid over my back. In the heat it was like adding butter to a frying pan.

I curled into a tight ball.

Drifted in and out of sleep.

Tired, so tired.

I thought of Louie racing over the rocks to get help, and how when everyone was struggling to get to higher ground after the waves, he'd gone the other way, not even thinking that more waves might come to kill him, or more ground might sink and take him down. Had those thoughts ever passed through his mind, even casually?

I shook my head. No . . . he's not like that. He doesn't stop to worry. He just does what he has to, like when he went to live in that warehouse. Louie has a problem, he works it out. He doesn't waste time thinking about it.

I slipped in and out of wakefulness.

Memories. Crazy thoughts.

Is this delirium?

Louie.

I half laughed to myself, thinking how I'd once been so terrified of him . . . him and the big guy smiling down on me with his foot on the wheel of my bike. *You scared, haole?* Louie in the dugout, beat up, crying.

Why was I remembering this?

I dozed and woke again to the same thoughts.

"Water," I croaked. My throat felt like sandpaper. I cupped a handful of warm salt water and brought it to my lips, licked at it and spat.

The sun spun above me.

And the big guy was there again, laughing, asking if I was afraid and saying, *You should be.* Then me, backing away, my pounding heart in my throat.

Louie charging me, his contorted face. *I'll get you!*

I remembered it all, shivering in the warm pool. If he'd caught up with me that day, Louie would have beaten me to a pulp.

My hand fell into the water. I let it stay there. It was so peaceful now.

No!

I slapped my face, tried to wake up.

Then sagged back . . . and slept.

"Senior patrol loser," someone said.

I peeked up. Louie and Mike were bending over the crevice, looking down.

"Heyyy," I croaked, then grimaced at the pain in my dried and cracked lips. I raised a hand to block the sun.

Louie squatted and lowered a canteen down to me by its strap. "Drink . . . but not too much . . . it's catchment water." He grinned.

So good to see that grin.

I took the canteen and struggled to my feet. I rubbed a hand over my face, hot water dripping off me.

Louie helped me get the cap off. "Forget the stink," he said. "It's water!"

"Is it boiled?"

"Nope."

It felt like liquid silk flowing down my throat. I drank deep. If it made me sick, so what? Better than dying. Louie took the canteen back and drank himself, then handed it to Mike. Mike sniffed it, made a face, and screwed the cap back on.

"Give some to Sam," Louie said.

Louie grabbed my hand and pulled me up out of the hole. We went over and looked down on Sam and Mr. Bellows. "We ain't the kind of help these two need," he said. He thought a moment. Working it out. One step after the other. "Okay, listen. First, we get um back with the other guys. After that, I going for help, find somebody with a phone."

"A phone?"

"Gotta be one somewhere."

"Be a miracle if there was."

Mike lifted the air mattress away and climbed down into Sam's depression. He crouched next to him, cradling his head. "Sammy boy . . . wake up. Drink some water. We're going home."

Mr. Bellows crawled out of his crevice, lifting the plywood away. I was so relieved—he was awake!

"Nice shelters," Louie said.

"All I could find."

"Next earthquake I hope I camping with you."

"Next earthquake I won't be anywhere near it."

Louie smirked. Mike handed him the canteen, and Louie took it over to Mr. Bellows.

Mike and I got Sam out of his hole. "Hey, Louie!" I tossed him his T-shirt and pulled mine over my head, my back itchy with drying salt.

Mr. Bellows folded the air mattress and held it to him as if it were a treasure. No way he was leaving it behind.

What am I doing? I'm not the one who needs protection. I took off my T-shirt and pulled it down over Sam. It fit him like a dress. "Okay," I said. "Let's go."

Louie nodded and gave me a thumbs-up.

We started the long, slow journey back to Halape.

23
WALKING
OUT

Louie, Mike, and I took turns carrying Sam. He couldn't walk on his own. Thankfully, Mr. Bellows could.

Masa headed down the slope the minute he spotted us coming around the point.

We limped closer.

"I sure am glad to see you," Masa said to Mr. Bellows as we met. "We thought the ocean swallowed you."

"It tried to." Mr. Bellows raised a hand to his head, then bent over. He put both hands on his knees. "Dizzy," he said. "I hit something hard . . . when . . . when . . ."

Masa put his hand on Mr. Bellows's back and turned to Louie, now carrying Sam. "How's the boy?"

"Too hot."

Masa nodded and turned back to Mr. Bellows. "Can you walk now?"

Mr. Bellows stood, grabbing Masa's arm for support. "Casey—"

"With us," Masa said. "He's okay."

Mr. Bellows closed his eyes in relief. "Zach?"

"Your boy found him. Scared, but no broken bones. Lots of cuts."

"Where was he?" I asked.

"Down the coast, opposite from where you went."

Good man, Casey, I thought. Especially with that knee. Wow.

"Come," Masa said, urging Mr. Bellows to keep moving. "We got a place for you. Everybody accounted for now. Nobody lost, nobody dead." His gaze slipped down. "Except for two horses . . . one was mine."

"I'm sorry," Mr. Bellows said.

Masa lifted his chin toward the hill. "We go."

Mike took Sam from Louie. We limped uphill, passing just above where our camp had been. I felt like I was hallucinating, still unable to grasp that the coconut grove was now in the ocean. I stepped over pieces of our old lives, stuff strewn everywhere. It looked as if a camping-gear factory had exploded.

"Wait," Louie said.

We stopped and watched as Louie leaped from rock to rock, heading toward the sea. He squatted to retrieve something, stood and squeezed the water out of it, then hopped back with Tad's blue blanket crumpled in his hand. Gear was scattered all over the place—tents, backpacks, valuable stuff— and he'd picked up Tad's blanket?

Billy wasn't crying or shouting out anymore, but he sat apart from everyone. The silver chain around his neck glinted in the sun. It made me sad just looking at him. His parents and his brother, Jesse, were probably going crazy worrying about him. This was Billy's first campout. I turned away.

"Zach!" I said, spotting him near Reverend Paia.

He looked up, empty-eyed.

I lifted my chin. "Good to have you back."

He nodded, but he didn't look so good. There was a long gash on his left upper arm. He didn't seem to notice it.

Mr. Bellows found a rock and sat on it bent forward with his head in his hands. Casey limped over on his stick cane and tried to hold a towel up to shade his dad. Mr. Bellows grabbed Casey's legs with one arm and hugged him close.

Louie and I squatted next to them, the blue blanket now draped over Louie's shoulder. "How you doing, sir?" Louie said. It startled me to hear him say *sir*. That word had never come out of him before.

Mr. Bellows looked up. He tried to smile. "Go help the others, Louie. I'll be all right."

"We take care of everything," Louie said. He glanced at me and jerked his head. We left.

Cappy and two paniolos huddled around Lenny, joking with him, trying to keep his spirits up. Lenny was hurting. He needed help, and soon.

Sam sat with a towel draped over his head. Masa was trying to make him a shelter with the air mattress. I bunched my lips. I should have hauled the piece of plywood back with us!

Too late now.

"Come," Louie said. He pulled the blanket off his shoulder and folded it neatly. Tad was hunched in the stingy shade of a clump of rocks and some towels. He was silent, gazing at the dirt. "Hey," Louie said, squatting down in front of him. "Look what I found."

Tad looked up, grabbed the blanket, and hugged it close. "Wet," he squeaked.

Louie grinned. "Sure is, brah, but you know what?"

Tad looked into Louie's eyes, his face cut and lumpy.

Louie turned and squinted up at the sun. "See that fireball? Dry um quick. . . . You like me spread it on the rocks for you?"

Tad nodded but wouldn't let go.

" 'S'all right. Dry quick even in your hands."

Tad buried his face in the blanket. Louie put his hand on his shoulder and stood.

We walked away. "That was nice," I said.

"He not going forget this day."

"Who will?"

We found Reverend Paia lying in the dirt, his good arm crooked over his eyes. Mike sat beside him. Someone put a hand on my shoulder and I turned. "We need more water," Masa said quietly.

"The catchment?"

"No more."

"It's empty?"

Masa nodded.

"How much we got left in the canteens?"

"Little bit."

Mike looked up. "How are we going to get out of here?"

I glanced up toward the trail we'd come in on. No way. Back down the coast where we'd planned to hike out was too far. In our condition it would take a week.

"The rangers know we're here," Masa said. "Somebody will come." Masa had lost his hat. A small bald spot sat on the back of his head.

"But *when*?" Mike said.

Masa tipped his head toward the mountain. "Depends on what happened up there, I guess. If the volcano blew, they won't be thinking of us."

"Someone will," I said, cringing at the thought of white-hot, slow-moving lava oozing down over the cliff. Where would we go? Into the ocean? "Did anyone see a flash of light over the sea last night?"

Masa nodded. "Looked like lightning."

"What was it?"

"Who knows?"

"It wasn't stormy," I said.

"No."

We stood a moment, looking out to sea. Some things were without explanation.

"I going get help," Louie said. "What if nobody thinking about us?"

"My mom is," I said.

Louie studied me, and I got the feeling that thinking of

his mother had never entered his mind. "Maybe. But we need help."

"I'm going with you," I said.

He nodded.

I grabbed a canteen, then thought twice. It was almost empty. I handed it to Masa.

"Take it," Masa said. "You need it in this heat."

"I can't leave my dad," Mike said.

"Yeah, me too," Casey said.

"No need," Louie said. "Zach," he called. "You and Tad watch Sam and Billy, ah? Can you do that?"

Zach nodded. He still looked dazed, but being around all of us seemed to help him unscramble his confusion.

Louie glanced at me. "Enough water in that canteen for two?"

I shook it. "A little less than half."

"How you going out?" Masa said. "Back up the trail?"

We looked uphill. It would be a long hike over a bad trail that was probably far worse now, if it was even there at all. Louie swept his gaze back to the coast, shimmering with heat. "We go this way. . . . Better."

"It's farther," Masa said.

"And safer," I said.

"Can't argue with that, but you boys watch where you step. Some places the lava is thin. . . . You can fall through."

Louie turned to me and raised his eyebrows.

"Let's move," I said.

"You don't have to go."

"I'm going."

Louie humphed. The old Louie was creeping back.

We started out. But Louie stopped and hopped the rocks back to Masa. "One thing," he said, looking Masa in the eye. "I was wrong, ah? To make fun of what you said about that shark."

Masa smiled and put a hand on Louie's shoulder.

Louie looked down, nodding.

We started toward the rocky shoreline. To get to the road we'd have to cross eleven miles of unbroken rock. It might be dark by the time we got there. Would anyone be driving on that road? Maybe it, too, had fallen into the sea.

Sweat rolled down from my temples. There was no breeze, and there probably never would be. This was a desolate place, made only for wasps and ants and roaches, creatures that could take a beating and survive.

I gazed into the distance. The coast went on forever. The road was somewhere down there in the haze, beyond anything we could see, maybe even beyond anything we could endure.

We'd find out.

24
BLOODY
FEET

For the first mile we snaked barefoot through low bushes, brown grass, and weeds. Louie took the lead. We didn't speak. The trail rose gently out of the sea-level bowl Halape sat in. It was easy going.

Until we hit the first lava flow.

The landscape turned to solid black rock. The trail was almost impossible to see, but you could make it out by following the *ahus,* or stacked stone markers that people had built to show the way. It was amazing that any were still standing after the earthquake. One stack led to the next, and to the next. The Hawaiians of long ago had come up with this idea. Reverend Paia said the common people weren't allowed to travel through the lush highlands, where it was cool, where it rained and sweet breezes blew. The highlands were *kapu,* off-limits, set apart for royalty. If a commoner got caught up there, it was the end of the line for that traveler.

Seemed like the end of the line down here, too.

There were two kinds of lava we would have to cross— smooth pahoehoe, and a'a, like shattered glass. Boots could take it. But our bare feet would be ground to raw meat.

Halfway across the first flow we stopped and gaped at what lay ahead. We were at the top of a rise in the land, the sun climbing into the sky directly in front of us. It reflected off the pahoehoe and nearly blinded me, the smooth rocks glistening endlessly into the distance, mile after mile after mile.

"Holy Moses," I whispered, shading my eyes and wishing I had a hat.

"Don't think about it," Louie said.

"Impossible."

"Okay, then think about how each step is taking you more close to the road."

"I might not live that long."

Louie shrugged. "How you look at it."

We limped on.

"How's your feet?" Louie said, stopping a moment.

"Sore."

"Going get more sore."

"We need wings."

I took the canteen from Louie. My tongue felt fat and dry. I took a sip and let the heavenly stink water sit in my mouth. The ocean to the right was blue, flat, and endless. Not one ripple marred its surface. When I turned and put the sun behind me, the color became even richer.

Then I remembered Sam.

And Reverend Paia's broken arm.

Casey's knee.

Lenny's head, floating in the water.

Mr. Bellows.

And how that colorful ocean was a fake . . . it had tried to kill me. I turned to hand the canteen back to Louie. "Let's move."

But Louie had already gone. I had to jog to catch up.

Our luck ended at a lava flow that had raced down over a previous flow. It was the fast kind—a'a, the kind that would rip our feet to shreds.

Louie inched ahead, testing his steps.

He stopped and stepped back. "I don't know."

I crept out onto the sharp rocks. "Jeese! How are we going to cross *this*?"

"Your shirt," he said. "Rip it in two, tie half to each foot."

"But the sun will cook us."

"No choice . . . 'less you can think of one."

I took my shirt off and tore it down the middle. My back was already fried. "No going back now."

"Nope."

Soon we had raglike T-shirt shoes. Looked like bandages. Louie took a step and grinned.

"While they last," I said.

"Go easy."

In less than an hour our shirt shoes were shredded and stained with blood. Louie stopped and pointed with his chin. Not far ahead the a'a ended. Smooth, sun-glazed pahoehoe lay like a carpet beyond.

"Yes!" I said.

But we both knew we hadn't seen the last of the bad stuff. I was seriously beginning to believe we were dreaming if we thought we could walk over any more a'a with only the rags on our feet.

Louie slipped the canteen off and took a sip to wet his caked lips. He handed it to me. "We think of something when we got to."

"All in the way you look at it."

Louie grinned. "You catching on, haole."

I drank a small amount and handed the canteen back. Louie shook it. "Going down fast."

"It does that when you drink it."

"You funny, for somebody going die of sunstroke."

I grunted.

We inched across the last few yards of ice-pick rock to the smooth pahoehoe and sat. I peeled the rags off my bloody feet. "Man, that stings."

Louie winced, his feet looking worse than mine.

The sun boiled down.

We rested, gazing at the desolation that surrounded us. Even the ocean looked desolate, because it couldn't help us.

"Let's go," Louie said. "Sit too long, we going get stiff."

"Stiff already."

"See?"

We staggered on.

"Hey, Louie," I said. "Did you hear those dogs last night? Before the earthquake?"

"No."

"They were howling, just like the night before."

He kept walking, then stopped and looked back. "They knew it was coming."

"You think so?"

"They were trying to warn us."

Could be, I thought. They'd howled from down the coast, and Masa said they didn't howl for nothing, and we'd gone that way and found Sam and Mr. Bellows. I was becoming a believer. Spirits, ghosts, howling dogs. The strange coincidence of Fred showing up and staying with Sam and Mr. Bellows until they were rescued.

It was creepy.

Or maybe it wasn't. All in the way you look at it, like Louie said. "Hey, you think that small white dog was Pele?" I asked.

"Sure."

"How come?"

"Because if I say it wasn't, then she going get mad and make my life miserable."

"Didn't she just do that?"

Louie snorted and kept walking.

We came upon a new flow, smooth, molten mud rock that had folded over itself, then dried and hardened.

We started out.

"Aiy!" Louie yelped, one foot breaking through the thin rock skin, then the other. He sat, then sank.

Vanished.

"Louie!"

He groaned.

I scrambled up and peeked over the edge of the hole. It

was dark. I could only see the top of his head. I got down flat on the lava, hanging over the edge. "Louie! Are you okay?"

He'd fallen into a tunnel, or a tube, where air had been trapped when the hot lava dried.

"Pull me up."

I reached down and grasped his hand. He was wedged in and had to wiggle his way out. I pulled him up. Blood oozed from a cut on his shin. "We need a stick so we can bang the rocks in front of us."

"Maybe we're not following the ahus."

"What ahus?" he said. "Look . . . no more."

He was right. Not one marker. We'd lost the path.

"Rest," Louie said, looking for a solid place to sit.

I stayed where I was, afraid to move and break the crust. I wasn't ready to visit the center of the earth.

The lonely coast wobbled in haze. Not one cloud sat in the endlessly blue sky. "It's too far, Louie."

He looked ahead, then back the way we'd come. "You think we halfway yet? Supposed to be eleven miles."

"Hard to tell."

We sat sizzling, bacon in a frying pan, our faces growing puffy from the heat. We were going to feel it in spades to-morrow. If there was a tomorrow.

I stretched my legs and massaged my calves. They were starting to tighten up. "Come on, we got to keep going."

He didn't move.

I shrugged. Who cared anymore? It was over. We had a thousand miles of broken glass to walk over on cut and bloody feet. We were done for.

I sat. In that heat it took everything I had left just to breathe. "We got two choices, Louie—get up and move on, or fry to death. Which one you like?"

He took a long time answering. "You think we going know it when we die? Or we just going fall asleep?"

I was still thinking about that when I heard the engine.

25
UNBELIEVABLE

"Chopper!" Louie shouted, struggling to his feet.

We got up and hobbled over the slight rise of the bowl we were in. Nothing in the sky.

But the sound was getting louder.

"There!" Louie said, jumping, waving his hands high above his head.

Skimming low along the coastline, a United States Coast Guard helicopter thumped toward us, the pulse of its rotors pounding the air. *Whup-whup-whup-whup!*

We leaped and waved and screamed, probably looking like fleas from the air. They could fly right over us and never know it.

"Here! Over here!"

"This way! Hey!"

They flew past. My heart pounded. "Come back!" My throat swelled with fire. Rescue passing us by was too much to take. "Wait . . ."

Louie jogged after them but soon gave up and stood watching them fade.

But the helicopter tilted and swooped in over the lava. "They saw us! Look, they saw us!"

The copter swung around and came back. For a moment it hovered over us, the pilot gazing down, talking into the mike on his helmet. I raised my arms, the wind from the rotors whipping up tiny bits of rock that stung my eyes.

Relief tumbled over me, a waterfall of everlasting love for the United States Coast Guard.

Whup-whup-whup-whup!

The sound was monstrous. I clamped my hands over my ears. The red and white colors of the coast guard never looked so good to me in all my life. The pilot hovered, searching for a place flat enough to land. The copter was huge, the size of two monster bulldozers. Red nose, white body, red tail. Three guys peered out the open side door.

I shielded my eyes as they crossed the blazing sun and came down smooth and settled on a patch of uneven rock.

We limped toward it, ducking into the wind of the rotors. A guy in an orange flight suit jumped out and jogged toward us. I nearly choked when I saw Dad in the doorway behind him. Never had that barrel chest and sea captain's scowl looked so good to me. He shouted and waved, but I couldn't hear over the roar of the rotors.

"Dad!" I yelled, overwhelmed to see him.

The man on the ground wore a helmet with a microphone

168

in it so he could talk with the pilot. It said *Ramos* on his flight suit. "You boys from the Scout group at Halape?" he shouted.

"Yes! We need help!"

"That's why we're here!" He motioned for us to hunch down.

Louie and I followed him to the helicopter. The blast from the rotors was fierce. Pieces of rock pricked my skin, like in a sandstorm.

Dad and another coast guard guy reached out to pull us up. "Thank God!" Dad shouted, hugging me close. He pushed me back and looked me over. "Are you all right?" he shouted.

"We need help! Mr. Bellows . . ." I gave up. It was too loud to talk.

Ramos motioned me toward a seat, shouting, "I'm going to strap you in!" Dad sat next to me. Louie settled across from us. Ramos buckled us in. "Ready, Cap," he said into his microphone.

Dad put his arm around my shoulder and hugged me again. I winced and he let go. "Bruises!" I shouted.

Dad nodded, deep creases in his face.

I glanced at Louie. "This is my dad! Dad, this is Louie!"

Louie nodded, then turned away. For the first time I noticed the gash behind his ear, the blood caked in his hair. Cuts and bruises raked his arms, legs, and face. Did I look as bad as he did?

"Hang on!" Ramos said. "We're going up!"

The engine roared.

I clutched the base of my seat as we rose, tipped, and sped toward Halape, the door on the starboard side wide open. Endless miles of black lava flew by below. From this height you could see the thin trail we'd been following, a faint gray snake on an endless black landscape. Another world, another universe. And there below was the spot where we'd drifted off onto the thin-crusted rock. I could see the hole Louie had fallen into.

The air cooled quickly.

The other coast guard guy, whose tag read *McCreedy*, tossed me and Louie coast guard T-shirts that he dug out of a box. I pressed mine against my burned face, feeling the heaven of something soft, something not of rock and heat. I put it on. He gave us water.

We drank deeply.

My eyes welled with thankfulness.

"How'd you get on this helicopter?" I shouted at Dad.

"Friends in coast guard! Got home last night!"

"Mom all right?"

He nodded. "Epicenter off Halape!"

"There was a wave!"

Dad motioned for me to wait, pointed at his ears. "Later!"

"Mister!" Louie shouted to Dad. "How big was it!"

"Seven point two!"

Louie and I glanced at each other.

We rode on without talking.

Dad watched the island pass by. I felt numb. Louie kicked my foot and lifted his chin to the open door. The helicopter was out over the water and circling back, banking. Halape came into view and you could see our small group looking up at us. All around them, and over the whole of Halape,

170

our gear was scattered like trash blown from a passing garbage truck. The small island offshore was mostly sunken, and the coconut grove grew up out of the ocean.

Louie looked back at me and shook his head.

I nudged Dad and pointed. "Some camped in those trees! I was in a shelter. . . . Gone now!"

We circled closer.

Dad studied the grove in the ocean, the crumbled shelters that had not been swallowed, the ragged survivors looking up at us like zombies. It was eerie the way they just stood there. Was something wrong?

Dad shook his head. "Unbelievable."

Tears filled my eyes.

Louie saw, his face fractured by my cracked lens. He turned away, showing none of the emotion I felt rushing up out of me. I took off my glasses and swiped at my eyes with the bottom of my T-shirt.

We landed close to the water where the sloping land flattened out. Two paniolos were off with the three remaining horses, soothing them as the helicopter settled.

Masa started down to us. No one else moved.

The engine slowed, the rotors swishing. We jumped out and ducked our way uphill. Why did everyone look like standing corpses? Was someone dead?

26
HEROES

Mr. Bellows lay in the dirt.

We ran up and knelt around him, Ramos and McCreedy with first-aid gear. They asked Casey to move aside and went to work. Ramos lifted Mr. Bellows's closed eyelids and checked his pupils, then listened to his chest and glanced up at McCreedy. "Weak."

"We thought we were losing him," Masa said.

"We did all we could," Reverend Paia said. Mike stood at his side, eyes empty.

Ramos looked up at Reverend Paia. "How long has this man been out?"

"An hour, maybe less."

"Come," Ramos said to Louie.

Louie got up and together they hurried down to the helicopter. McCreedy stayed with Mr. Bellows. "You his son?" he asked Casey, and Casey nodded. "He'll be all right," McCreedy said. "I'm sure of it."

Casey closed his eyes and took a deep breath.

Ramos and Louie came back with a stretcher and, along with McCreedy, eased Mr. Bellows onto it. McCreedy needled a tube into Mr. Bellows's arm. The tube ran up to a bag of liquid. McCreedy handed the bag to me. "Hold this above his body."

Casey, Louie, and I followed them down to the helicopter and got Mr. Bellows settled in the cabin. Ramos radioed for medical instructions.

"Case," I said. In that moment I felt a million miles away from him. I didn't know what to say. I put my hand on his shoulder. He was trembling. "You okay?"

He nodded.

But he wasn't. I could feel his terror.

McCreedy's eyes were blue and comforting. "Don't worry," he said. "We'll get him to a hospital as quick as we can."

"Stay with him," Ramos said to McCreedy, then tapped me and motioned toward another stretcher. I gave Casey's shoulder a squeeze and jumped out after Ramos. McCreedy and Louie handed down the stretcher. I limped uphill.

Back up at the gathering site, Mike and Reverend Paia with his one good arm were picking things up, getting everyone ready to head to the helicopter.

Dad squatted with Masa and Cappy, trying to help

Lenny. The other two paniolos were still with the horses. They'd recovered all five saddles.

Ramos dropped down next to Masa. Dad moved aside as Ramos went to work to stabilize Lenny's broken bones. Lenny was pale, his humor gone.

I turned and saw Louie and Casey slowly making their way over the rocks with another stretcher. Casey'd tossed his cane, taking the pain in his knee. It was good to see him up and moving. Worrying wasn't doing him any good.

Slowly, we managed to get everyone into the helicopter. We all drank water.

Louie and I jumped out with Masa and took canteens to the two paniolos with the horses. Masa's plan was that Cappy would go with Lenny in the helicopter, and the three of them would take the horses back up the trail, hoping there was enough trail left to make it to the top. From there they'd ride up to the Volcano House and call the ranch for a horse truck.

Masa handed the two paniolos canteens. They drank, then poured some into their hands for the horses.

"You think there's much of a trail left?" Masa said.

"If no got, we make um," one of them said.

Masa turned to me and Louie. "You boys come up and see us sometime, okay? We friends now, us. So you come. We put you on a couple horses and take you to places people rarely see."

"Yeah," I said. "We'll do it."

Louie nodded.

Masa pointed at him. "For sure, ah?"

Louie put a hand on his heart. We'd never forget what we shared here at Halape.

Masa grinned and touched his forehead with two fingers in salute. The paniolos mounted and headed out, picking their way up the trail, Masa sitting straight in his saddle.

Minutes later, the copter lifted off and left Halape behind.

A nightmare, fading.

Flying out, we huddled like the wounded being evacuated from a war zone. We were lucky. It could have been a whole lot worse.

The landscape passed by below. The desolate coast, the scorched scrub brush, the fingers of black lava that snaked down from the mountains and spread to the sea. What had been a disaster for us was, for the island, nothing more than a yawn, a stretch, a shrug.

Louie seemed to notice it, too. Or maybe what we'd just been through was starting to sink in, the what-could-have-beens, the what-ifs. He sat across from me, strapped in and facing away from the cut-up and broken bodies spread out on the deck around us.

What was he thinking?

I was trying to imagine the answer when I realized how much I'd been thinking about Louie Domingo.

I took off my glasses and wiped the lenses on my T-shirt. I put them back on and closed one eye. A cracked and fuzzy

Louie sat across from me. I closed that eye and opened the other. Crystal clear.

He lifted his chin, What?

I tapped my glasses and mouthed Thanks over the din of the engine.

He held up four fingers and pointed to his eyes—four eyes.

I tapped my butt and my head, then pointed at him.

He grinned and turned away.

Dad tapped my leg, not looking at me, just tapping, as if to say I'm so thankful.

Yeah, I thought. Me too.

I pulled a foot up and studied it. Blood and dirt were caked in and around a field of raw cuts, which were stinging more now that I had time to think about it. Ramos tossed me a pack of disinfectant wipes and a roll of gauze. I made another pair of cloth shoes. Not bad. I tossed the wipes and gauze to Louie.

Mr. Bellows lay nearby, still unconscious. Or maybe, I hoped, he was just asleep. Yes, he was just sleeping. Nothing is going to happen to Mr. Bellows. It can't.

Casey sat silently beside him. Anyone could read his thoughts. Because they were the same for all of us—Nothing is going to happen, he'll be fine, we'll all be fine. Including busted-up Lenny, who lay on a stretcher, joking again. Joking! And he was worse off than anyone. Those paniolos must eat spurs for breakfast. Or else McCreedy gave him something to take away the pain.

I thought back to the moment we'd swept up and headed away from Halape. Looking down, I'd seen the horses climbing up the steep slope, another image I'd carry with me awhile. Already I missed Masa, and even the two paniolos I hadn't gotten to know. Halape hadn't killed anyone, but it could have. When people share something terrifying like that, it joins them together and makes them a family. Like Masa said, *We friends now.*

Friends.

"Take it slow, Masa," I whispered, remembering how even before the earth shook it had been a dangerous trail. "Nice and slow."

27
HOME

We came down in a quiet corner of Hilo Airport, away from the terminal. It was around four in the afternoon. Two ambulances and a small crowd were waiting for us in a roped-off area on the tarmac. I could see Mom and Dana's blond heads. Mrs. Bellows was there. And Mike's mom. Sam's parents. Billy's, Zach's, Tad's, and all their brothers and sisters, and people I didn't know, including guys with cameras.

But I saw no one who looked like they might be there for Louie. He knew it would be that way. He didn't even try to look for anyone. His face was as blank as the first day he came to Scouts.

The pilot shut the engine down. The crowd was held

back by a rope attached to two temporary posts as the ambulance crew hurried toward us with rolling stretchers.

I unbuckled and stood. Mom saw me and waved, Dana beside her, stretching over the crowd to see. I gave them an okay sign. Mom's face flushed with relief. Dana put her arm around her.

Someone dropped the rope and the crowd broke and rushed the helicopter.

Ramos and Louie lowered Tad, Billy, and Zach to the tarmac. One of the medics began checking them over. The bruises and the cuts and gashes that slashed their arms and faces made people gasp and huddle close to them. Sam's mom squeezed toward us, looking scared to death over not seeing Sam get off.

Mike jumped out and helped his father down.

Sam, Mr. Bellows, Casey, Cappy, and Lenny waited in the hold. Louie, Dad, and I stayed behind to help. Three medics scrambled aboard and broke out their equipment.

Down on the tarmac I could hear Sam's mother screaming. "Sam! Sam!" Reverend Paia caught her, saying, "He's all right! Don't worry. Let the medical crew do their work. He'll be out soon."

Dad and I helped Casey to the tarmac. The bandage on his knee was the size of a small watermelon. He limped badly.

The medics secured Sam and Mr. Bellows to stretchers and lowered them out of the hold.

Mrs. Bellows found Casey and hugged him. Casey looked over her shoulder at me and Louie, still in the helicopter. He wanted to say something but couldn't find the words. Mrs. Bellows let him go and huddled over Mr. Bellows.

Casey hobbled back to us. "Listen," he said, but didn't continue.

"Your dad going be fine, brah," Louie said, squatting in the cabin, looking down at Casey. "You better go. They taking him away."

Casey limped to catch up as the medics rolled Mr. Bellows toward one of the ambulances. Casey's sprouting red hair was as tangled as I'd ever seen it.

A medic climbed into the cabin and quickly checked me and Louie over. "You boys have these cuts and bruises cleaned up, all right? Go to your doctor or come up to the hospital. Today, soon as you can. You have to be concerned about infection."

"Sure," I said, but I'd almost forgotten that I had them. They didn't sting anymore. Maybe tomorrow they would, but not now. Louie elbowed me and dipped his chin toward Zach, who was keeping close to Billy and Tad while they made their way to their parents. Being a buddy.

Dad put a hand on my shoulder. "You ready?"

"Yeah, sure." I paused and glanced toward Louie, now with his back to us, staring out at the crowd. "Hey, Louie . . . you had enough of this?"

He turned and nodded.

"Let's go, then."

We jumped off and made our way into the crowd. Cameras flashed as the medics began rolling the stretchers to the ambulances.

Dad shook hands with Ramos, McCreedy, and the pilot. "Thank you" was all he could say.

"You saved us," I added.

"That's what we do, kid," the pilot said.

We headed toward the crowd, Dad craning his neck. "You see Dana and your mom?"

"They were with Mrs. Bellows . . . over there, Dad."

Mom looked up and I waved.

She squeezed toward us, Dana following. "Dylan!" Mom said. "Oh, honey!" She hugged me so tight I thought my bones would snap.

"I'm okay, Mom, I'm okay."

Dana scowled at the cuts on my arms. She looked as clean as a marshmallow.

Mom pushed me back. "Your face, your glasses!" she said, tears streaming down her cheeks. "These cuts! Don't you *ever* do this to me again!"

"Next time," Dad said, "I'm going to tag along."

I looked at him, then smiled. "Anytime, Dad."

Louie stood nearby, looking up at the faces gazing out the terminal windows. He turned, nodded to me, then limped off.

"Mom," I said, trying to break away.

Dad understood. He peeled Mom away from me and pulled her to him. "Dylan's got something to do."

"You come right back!" she said.

"Louie!" I shouted, dodging my way through the crowd. My feet stung, making me wince. "Louie, wait up!"

He ignored me, weaving away unsteadily.

"Louie!"

181

I caught up and grabbed his arm. "Slow *down*. We can give you a ride."

He stopped and stared at my hand. I let go.

"I don't need no ride," he said.

"What do you mean? Look at your feet! Jeese, look at mine. We're crippled. It's just a ride."

"I said I don't need it." He limped on.

I kept up with him. So stubborn. What happened to the new Louie, the good one? Now we had to go back to the old one? "Come on. Haven't you beaten yourself up enough already? You can't walk home on those feet and you know it."

He kept going.

"Okay," I said, a step behind him. "We'll do it your way. Where to?"

That stopped him. "Whatchoo want, haole? Ah? Explain me that."

"Nothing . . . I just . . . well, we just . . ."

He snorted and started limping faster.

Now I was getting angry. "You don't stop, sucka, I going broke your stupid ugly face and mess you up good!" I held up my fists.

Louie turned back. He tried not to grin. Then it vanished. "Whatchoo care?"

I dropped my hands. "It's a ride, big deal. To the doctor. And anyway . . . I know something about you now."

"Yeah?"

"Yeah . . . I know you're not the scary punk you want me to think you are."

"Well, you still a four-eyed dork."

I grinned. "So?"

Louie puffed his cheeks, looked down. Then up.

"You're coming with us," I said.

"Okay, fine . . . but one condition."

"What?"

"We stop at the hospital, see Mr. Bellows."

"For sure, for sure. And get our feet cleaned up while we're there. Then buy some Band-Aids and rubber slippers."

Louie leaned and spat, then bumped past me, heading back. "This don't mean nothing, ah?"

"Not a thing."

"Good."

"Yeah, good."

I walked behind him.

Ahead, Sam's gurney rolled toward us, heading to the ambulance. Sam's dad walked next to it. Louie hobbled over to them. "Sammy boy," he said. "How you doing?"

Sam peeked up at him, barely conscious.

Louie grabbed his hand, thumb to thumb, man style. "I come see you tomorrow, little man. You more strong than all of us, ah? A survivor. You did good, brah."

A small smile crept onto Sam's face.

"While you sleeping I going check if the Boy Scouts got one Purple Heart badge." He rested his hand on Sam's shoulder. "Take care, ah?"

"Thank you," Sam's dad said. Louie nodded. The medics headed Sam over to the ambulance.

Louie glanced at me. "Whatchoo looking at? I thought we was going get slippers."

"I got a question."

"You wasting my time."

"Remember that day you wanted to kill me?"

Louie hesitated, trying to figure out what I was talking about. Then it clicked. His eyes narrowed.

"Who was that big guy and what did you have that he wanted?"

Louie stepped closer. "You no like go there, haole."

"Yeah . . . I do. That guy told me I should be scared of him."

"He did?"

"He was spooky. He laughed after he said it."

Louie studied the ground, his hand on the back of his neck. He shook his head and smirked. "That was Luke . . . my brother."

"Your *brother* beat you up? Why?"

"I had his switchblade knife. I stole it from him. I wanted to be bad, like him. But he wouldn't let me. That's why he was beating me up . . . taking back that knife, making sure I didn't turn out like him. He was watching out for me." He looked off and added, "Still he does."

Wow, I thought. Did I have *that* wrong.

"But he's in jail right now."

I let that sit a moment. "That's . . . I'm sorry."

"Yeah."

I hesitated, then said, "You . . . you recognized me the minute you saw me in the Bellows's garage, didn't you?"

He grinned.

"So how come you never said anything?"

He shrugged. "Why? That day was about me and my brother, not you."

This was Louie Domingo talking?

184

"Listen," he said, coming closer. "You know why I give you hard time?"

"Why?"

"Because you so *stupid*."

I scowled.

"But I going stop giving you hard time now. You know why?"

I looked at him.

He stuck out his hand to shake, thumb to thumb. I took it. He squeezed, hard. "You got guts, that's why."

I gaped at him.

He dropped my hand. "We go, haole."

"Wait . . . uh . . . are you . . . are you going to stay in Scouts? I know Mr. Bellows made you come."

He smirked. "Nobody can make me do what I don't want to do, punk."

It took me a second to get it. "Good," I said, nodding. "Good."

"You was going buy me slippers, remember?" He grinned and walked away, motioning for me to follow.

What? I'm his dog now?

He moved through the crowd, shaking a hand, patting a back. Smiling.

An ambulance headed out with its lights flashing, and I caught a glimpse of Casey in the back window with his dad. Was Sam in there, too? I cringed, thinking of how we'd almost lost them. The luckiest thing Mr. Bellows ever did in his life was walk into that vacant warehouse.

I squinted at Louie Domingo through my mangled glasses.

And limped after him.

AUTHOR'S NOTE

Wave heights from the Nov. 29 tsunami ranged from as low as four feet off Waiakea Peninsula in Hilo to 20 feet at points in Ka'u. . . . There were at least five waves in the series produced by the strong offshore quake, the most intense in Hawaii in more than a century.
— Honolulu Advertiser, *Friday, December 12, 1975*

Night of the Howling Dogs is a work of fiction based on the true events of November 29, 1975. Six Boy Scouts and four adult leaders from Troop 77 of Hilo, Hawaii, had set up a weekend camp at Halape, a remote beach campground on the southern flank of Kilauea volcano. In the black predawn the Scouts suddenly found themselves caught up in an unimaginable fight for their lives. My cousin Tim Twigg-Smith was one of them.

Though the characters and personal situations in *Night of the Howling Dogs* are my own inventions, the geological events of that weekend happened as they happen in this book . . . and like Dylan, Tim in real life let go of his glasses just when he thought his end had come.

The magnitude 7.2 earthquake, the largest in Hawaii since the 7.9 quake of 1868, caused the south coast of the Big Island to drop nearly twelve feet into the ocean. The sudden sinking generated a tsunami that rushed inland over the campers an astonishing three hundred feet and rose fifty feet above sea level.

Though slashed, battered, and nearly drowned, Tim and his fellow Scouts survived. But one of their adult leaders, Dr. James Mitchel, was lost in the quake-generated rockslide from the cliff above. A fisherman, Michael Cruz, who'd ridden down to Halape on horseback from Keeau, was swept out to sea and never found.

Five years after that nightmare, I asked Tim if he would consider hiking back down to Halape to show me around and spend the night. I was fascinated by his story and wanted to see the place for myself, especially the coconut trees rising out of the ocean from where the old campground now sat—underwater.

Amazingly, Tim agreed.

A few months later, with Tim and his brother, Michael, I hiked down to Halape along the rugged eight-mile trail from the Hilina Pali trailhead.

Like Dylan in *Night of the Howling Dogs,* I was captured

by the peace and pristine beauty of Halape. I swam in the crack, dodged stinging ants and flying roaches, sat on the rocks, and soaked in the cool blue ocean. I boiled and drank stinky catchment water and explored the rocky coast. I was truly amazed, and silently thanked Tim for having the courage to return again to camp under the looming cliff of Pu'u Kapukapu.

That night we unrolled our sleeping bags on the sand and slept under the stars, the ocean whispering not far away. The air was warm, and the Milky Way raced across the universe, as clear and bright as you could ever hope to see it.

But sleep didn't come easily.

I couldn't help thinking: What if . . .

An hour before sunrise the next morning we packed our gear, savaged down a can of peaches, saving one more for later, and began the long hike out to Chain of Craters Road, eleven sizzling miles down the desolate coast.

Two hours later the sun was trying to kill us. My feet were blistered and swelling in my boots. I stank of sweat. There was absolutely no shade. We stopped and sat in silence, too hot to talk.

Michael dropped his backpack and searched for something to eat. Tim squeezed into an eighteen-inch fissure, trying to escape the heat.

We got up and moved on.

Tim took the lead, setting a gruesome pace.

At one point Michael and I stopped to split a Snickers bar. That's when I learned about the wasps, and how wild they could get over something sweet. We ran for our lives, swatting them away with our hats.

Tim was now a blip in the hazy distance. Michael and I had to hustle to catch up.

Eventually, mercifully, we made it to the road. But our prearranged ride wasn't there. The road was deserted—no cars, no shade, no spigot of clear, cool water, no green grass to lie down on.

Rock and blacktop. That was it.

We sat; sooner or later someone would come.

Michael took out the last can of peaches and pried it open with his pocketknife. We divided it up.

Nothing.

Ever.

Tasted.

So.

Good.

Thank God for peaches.

For a second I thought about thanking Tim, too, for having the guts to return to Halape. But I decided to do that later. Right then all he cared about was water, shade, and maybe a cool breeze.

We were never near death that day as we sat dehydrating in the sun, but we were close enough that I could imagine it. Truly, that moment helped me appreciate what I am: a miraculous living being, part of all life around me. Everything fit together like a tight puzzle, and we had to take care of each other.

Just as our last drop of water ran out, our ride showed up.

Photo by Dorothy Thompson

The Scouts and leaders who camped at Halape in 1975 (left to right):
Fal Allen, David White, Don White (David's father), Dr. James
Mitchel, Jimmy Kawakami (a Honolulu policeman), Leaf Thompson,
Claude Moore, Michael Sterns, Tim Twigg-Smith, Noel Loo.

GRAHAM SALISBURY'S family has lived in the Hawaiian Islands since the early 1800s. He grew up on Oahu and Hawaii and graduated from California State University. He received an MFA from Vermont College of Norwich University, where he was a member of the founding faculty of the MFA program in writing for children. He lives with his family in Portland, Oregon.

Graham Salisbury's books have garnered many prizes. *Blue Skin of the Sea* won the Bank Street Child Study Association Award and the Oregon Book Award; *Under the Blood-Red Sun* won the Scott O'Dell Award for Historical Fiction, the Oregon Book Award, Hawaii's Nene Award, and the California Young Reader Medal; *Shark Bait* won the Oregon Book Award and a *Parents' Choice* Silver Honor; *Lord of the Deep* won the *Boston Globe–Horn Book* Award for fiction. *Jungle Dogs* was an ALA Best Book for Young Adults; *Island Boyz: Stories* was a *Booklist* Editors' Choice; and *Eyes of the Emperor* was an ALA Best Book for Young Adults and a *Kirkus Reviews* Best Book of the Year and won the Oregon Book Award. Graham Salisbury's most recent book is *House of the Red Fish.*

Graham Salisbury has been a recipient of the John Unterecker Award for Fiction and the PEN/Norma Klein Award. You can visit him at his Web site, www.grahamsalisbury.com.